A Not So Simple Seminar

Holt Jacobs Mystery - Book 5

Lily Stirling

~ To Miss Crystal ~

Thanks for inspiring excellence on and off the dance floor.

CONTENTS

CHAPTER 1

"I can't believe you wanted to live in Arizona," I said, critically observing the Camelback Hotel's decor as I waited to get checked in.

My girlfriend, Brittany, shook her head. "Nope. Not buying it. You don't actually hate Phoenix, Arizona."

I raised an eyebrow. "I don't?"

She took a step closer, and the scent of her black hair distracted me from the fact I was supposed to be skeptical. Clearing my throat, I asked, "What's your proof?"

"For starters," Brittany said, her eyes sparkling, "when you told me about the work trip, you complained about *leaving* Seattle, not about *going* to Phoenix."

"That's pretty thin," I said. "A jury's not going to convict with that."

"I'm not finished," Britt said. "Second, I didn't hear you groan once in the Phoenix airport, on the ride over, or even when we entered the hotel."

"Hey! I don't go around groaning about everything I dislike."

Britt continued. "Your mood only turned sour after your boss dragged you away to talk to those people."

"What's your point?"

My question was more clipped than intended. Still, I hadn't gotten over Rick making me shake hands with executives the moment I'd walked into Camelback Hotel. My messenger bag had been slung over my shoulder and my suitcase was rolling beside me. I remained professional during introductions, but I died on the inside. Rick hadn't even let me check in before parading me about like I was the heifer who'd just won the blue ribbon at the county fair.

"My point is you're mad at Rick, which has nothing to do with Phoenix."

I stared at her, unwilling to admit she was right.

"What is he making you do?" she asked. "I thought you liked working for him."

I shrugged. "I messed up by solving a problem right before the conference. Rick's planning on making me a celebrity."

Thankfully, it was my turn at the front desk, so Britt let the matter drop. Once I had my key card, I was about to rejoin my buddy Darren and my baby sister, Juniper, when Britt grabbed my arm. "Wait," she said. "I'm not sure about this."

"Britt, this'll—"

She interrupted. "Don't you dare smirk at me."

I shook my head. "Nothing to smirk about."

That was a lie. Brittany had made the mistake of saying "I'm jealous Holt's going to Arizona" while on a group call with my sister. Juniper had decided to *surprise* Britt by planning an Arizona girls' weekend at a spa near the conference center.

Supposedly, Juniper's such a popular social media personality that the spa agreed to let Juniper and a guest stay for free as long as she filmed clips of the spa during the trip. Plus, Juniper's husband is frequently gone on business trips, and she's always on the lookout for her own adventures.

Britt wasn't overly excited about spending a long weekend with my over-the-top sister. Yet she hadn't figured out a polite way to decline. Which is how my girlfriend ended up in Phoenix the same weekend as my work conference.

Though it makes me a bad boyfriend, I found the whole thing hilarious. Juniper was always making me do things I didn't want to. For once, someone else was the target.

Once we rejoined the other two, Darren asked, "Ready to drop off our luggage?" He'd checked in while my boss was introducing me to the blur of executive faces.

Originally, Darren and I were supposed to share a generic two-queen bedroom, but since I'd had the misfortune of making a major breakthrough shortly before the conference, I was being given all-star treatment, and my room had been upgraded.

"I'm all set," I answered.

"Good," Darren said. "I grabbed our welcome bags." He nodded toward a foldout table that had been set up with a banner proclaiming ENGINEERS OF THE FUTURE IN THE PRESENT. It was a pretentious mouthful. I'll never understand why so many organizations send their employees to this annual conference.

There was a decent number of attendees who worked at engineering firms but weren't engineers. Like Darren's a lawyer, yet he was expected to attend, because really the conference was an excuse to make new contacts, with plenty of time set aside for individual organizations to run their own team-building programs. Pretty much a nightmare.

Darren was already wearing an ENGINEERS OF THE FUTURE IN THE PRESENT lanyard complete with his full name, job title, and the organization we worked for. I dug my conference badge out of the welcome bag.

I stared at the badge. At my job, my goal had been to play with cool things. My sudden fame was unexpected and unwelcome. Once I put on the lanyard, everyone would know I was the famous Holt Jacobs who worked for BECKS.

I'm not sure what BECKS stands for. I should probably know, seeing as they pay me, yet the only thing I'm confident about is that the *E* in BECKS stands for *Engineering*.

Darren noticed my hesitation. "You have to wear it."

I nodded and slipped the lanyard over my head. It was a noose sealing my doom.

"Now you're official," Britt said.

"I guess so." I did my best not to grumble.

Juniper tilted her head. "Yeah, I'm totally jealous you get to go to this cool work conference while I'm stuck relaxing at a five-star spa."

I rolled my eyes. "How ever will you survive?" Though, really, a weekend seminar might be awful, but at least it didn't involve strangers touching me. "And when are the two of you leaving for your spa place?" I glanced nervously in my boss's direction. I didn't want Rick exaggerating my accomplishments to Britt or Juniper. The sooner they cleared out, the better.

"Soon," Juniper said, waving her hand like it was nothing. Chouzie, her midsized chow chow, gave a bark of agreement from his spot at her feet. For once my sister wasn't suspicious of my behavior, but Brittany's face was her professional paramedic mask, and she was analyzing me for clues.

The only reason they hadn't gone straight to the spa was because Camelback Hotel was a massive event center, with a full-size auditorium, many meeting rooms, and at least three restaurants. Juniper claimed she needed to check out the food options. Though so far all she'd done was hang out with us in the lobby.

Somehow I missed Rick sneaking up, but suddenly he was back, shaking hands with my girlfriend. "Brittany, good to see you." After Britt made some sort of polite reply, Rick was clapping me on the back. "Geoff Hodges had a family emergency and will be flying out tonight."

Who's Geoff?

Instead of asking about Geoff, I nodded.

"He still wants to give his showcase and has time before the flight. Can we move your speech to the closing night, and he'll take today's spot?"

"Of course," I said, ignoring the growing heat on my face. As soon as I'd answered, Rick was off bothering someone else. But the damage was done.

"You got a public speaking gig?" Juniper asked, like I was moonlighting to become the next Tony Robbins.

"Not exactly," I said, wishing I could disappear to my room, but there was no way Juniper would let me off the hook without some sort of explanation. "I was told—*not asked*, told—to give a presentation on some recent discoveries."

Darren actually snorted at that. "I had no idea you were so modest."

Please, don't.

"Holt's modest?" Juniper rested a manicured finger on her lips.

"These discoveries must be important if you're giving a speech about them," Brittany said with a hint of sadness in her voice.

Darren said, "Holt simplified an issue that will save BECKS millions of dollars each year. Of course they want to show him off."

Britt and Juniper eyed me curiously.

"In a way that piece was like your appendix—easily removed with no decrease in functionality." I tried to downplay it. "No big deal. It's a fifteen-minute showcase." I shrugged. "I'm just a guy who likes playing with cool things."

"Yeah," Darren said, choosing not to be helpful. "It's no big deal. Just eight major companies coming together to showcase their best and brightest, and they asked Holt to speak."

I shot Darren a *You'd better shut up* glare.

Britt asked, "Why didn't you tell me?"

Fidgeting with my dress shirt's collar, I said, "I did...sort of."

"Sort of?" Juniper asked. "What's *sort of*?"

Everyone was watching me. I ran a self-conscious hand through my hair. "The night we went to that weird found footage movie, you asked how my day was and I said, *Good. I just solved a problem at work.*"

"Oh" was what Britt said, but the little scar by her eyebrow was outlined.

She wasn't thrilled with my answer.

I shrugged. "People are just excited right now because it's something new to talk about. I'm a shiny toy that'll be forgotten in a few days."

"A shiny toy that got a bigger office, a sizable raise, and a huge bonus," Darren added.

"Well..." I tried to hide my grin since I was annoyed with Darren, but the bonus had been nice.

Brittany was still troubled, and Juniper seemed skeptical that her brother could accomplish anything noteworthy.

"Can we watch your showcase?" Juniper asked. From her tone, she clearly expected that my attempt at public speaking would be a train wreck.

"No watching," I said.

"Sure," Darren said with an innocent smile. "I'm sure the organizers would encourage supportive friends and family cheering on their speakers."

I shook my head. "Absolutely not."

Darren shrugged. "All the showcases are being recorded. I'll let you watch the replay on my work account."

Juniper squealed, while I considered finding different friends.

Suddenly my boss was back. "Geoff's showcase starts in fifteen minutes. You'd better hurry if you want to drop off your luggage."

"Sure thing." I doubt Rick heard, since he'd already walked away.

"Yeah, we'd better hurry," Darren said. "Can't have Holt missing his afternoon nap."

"His what?" Juniper asked, her eyes widening in anticipation.

Seriously? Why was Darren bent on sharing all my secrets as fast as possible?

"He hasn't told you?"

Juniper shook her head, and Darren leaned in like he was about to share something scandalous. "You see," Darren said very seriously, "when people are giving speeches, Holt is an expert at finding the dimmest, most abandoned seat in the auditorium, and then he'll sleep through them."

"Hey!" I tried to sound outraged. "I would never sleep during something important. I meditate in deep contemplation."

"Oh." Juniper giggled. "Darren, do you also 'meditate in deep contemplation'?"

He shook his head. "I would, but when I meditate as deeply as Holt does, I snore."

Juniper gave me a shove. "Some guys get all the luck."

"You don't take it seriously?" Britt's words felt cold, and even Juniper and Darren flinched.

"I mean..." I tried to come up with a diplomatic answer. "Just the boring ones."

I winced. *Why had I said that?*

"Seminars that actually pertain to me, I take very seriously. But"—I shoved my hands into the pockets of my slacks—"they bring in these business gurus who know nothing about our company, let alone my engineering division, and all they do is prance around onstage throwing out buzzwords about how 'we need to synergize our options to increase more visibility...'" I shook my head. "It's a waste of time."

"And you're okay with this?" she asked Darren.

He shrugged. "Holt would be falling asleep whether he tried to or not. At least with me there, no one's catching him."

"I see," Britt said, but her face was expressionless.

This wasn't good.

I widened my eyes at Juniper, using nonverbal sibling code to ask what I'd done wrong. Her raised eyebrows seemed to say, *How should I know?*

There was probably an awkward silence forming when Darren announced, "We really have to toss our bags in our rooms right now or we'll be late."

"Yeah, Brittany and I have a foot soak scheduled. We'd better get to the spa," Juniper said.

I followed Darren to the elevators, but I couldn't help watching Britt leave. She wasn't happy with me, but was it from not sharing enough about my big discovery, sleeping through speeches, or both?

I stayed with Darren as he went to his room on the seventh floor. I had to make sure I sat next to him when the seminar started. The key to sleeping through speeches is to have a trustworthy companion who will both shield you from other people and wake you up when it's over.

Once I'd been abandoned in the back of a bus during a high school trip after falling asleep in the back row. No one remembered to get me.

When I woke up, the bus was parked at the hotel, it was the middle of the night, and I was starving.

Darren's hotel room was what you'd expect. Two beds and a bathroom. Aside from the art being cactus themed, there was nothing to differentiate this room from any other chain hotel room across the nation.

My upgrade was definitely an upgrade. First off, it was on the twentieth floor. I don't know why a higher floor means fancier...If you think about it, you're more likely to die in a fire or an earthquake. Still, higher floor equals fancier. Second, it was far away from the elevator with its constant dinging and foot traffic. My room was on a side hallway beside a stairwell. Given it's the twentieth floor, I'm guessing not too many people take the stairs.

Instead of a dim entryway with a bathroom to one side, the door opened into a living room flooded with natural light. Off to one side was globe lighting over a kitchen peninsula. My first few apartments weren't as nice as this place.

Darren let out a low whistle. "Nice digs."

The bathroom had a huge walk-in shower plus a large whirlpool bathtub.

I was about to enter the master bedroom when Darren took me by the shoulder. "Nope. If you go in there, you'll take a nap in the bed instead of in the drafty auditorium. Let's go."

He was right. I'd much rather sleep on a super-expensive mattress. The last time I slept through a presentation, I woke up with a horrible crick in my neck.

Once we returned to the lobby, we walked with a tide of mostly strangers and some vaguely familiar faces who were all more or less dressed in relaxed business clothes, wearing lanyards proclaiming they were attendees of ENGINEERS OF THE FUTURE IN THE PRESENT.

Darren didn't have a suit coat on, but he wore a tie over his button-up. As for me, I wore a suit, but I'd skipped the tie and left my top button undone.

I took the lead when it came to choosing seats. As Darren mentioned, there was an art to finding a seat where you could nap unnoticed. After a couple of near hits, I finally found the perfect spot and settled into my seat.

Now, falling asleep before the talk starts is a rookie mistake. Only do this if you want to get caught. Plenty of people are moving around, and usually the auditorium lights are on.

Sighing, I checked my phone. Nothing from Brittany, but my sister had sent a photo to the family group text of two fancy blended adult beverages, so they must've made it to the spa.

What could I say to Brittany? She was upset when they left, but was there a way to fix it? Finally I sent: *Hope your spa's as awesome as my upgrade.* I'd just pressed send when the lights dimmed and the chatter around me died down.

I was a good boyfriend (though a bad employee), because I watched my phone until Britt replied. All she'd done was *heart* my message, which could mean anything. I waited another minute, and when nothing else came, I put away my phone, crossed my arms, and bowed my head.

Worrying about Britt wouldn't get me anywhere, and I had a nap to take. I'd just drifted off when Darren elbowed me. "Holt, he's choking."

Thankfully, I had the presence of mind to keep silent as I woke up—I really didn't want to be known as the man who started complaining loudly in crowded auditoriums.

"What?" I asked when I could trust myself to talk quietly.

"Geoff's choking up there."

Darren had woken me up for that?

After rubbing my eyes, I finally focused on the stage. The top of the man's balding head was shiny from sweat, and he seemed to be having trouble speaking. "...the goal of...of synergistification is..."

"That's not a word," I whispered.

"See," Darren said. "This is a show worth watching."

Though I wasn't sure it was worth waking me up for, the speech was a level of train wreck I had yet to experience.

"...and what...what are we missing?" Mr. Speaker kept going, but his face had gone bright red, he was blinking rapidly, and he was moving strangely around the stage.

Wait.

Had he been poisoned?

Wow. Can you say overactive imagination?

This guy could be experiencing stage fright, the brown bottle flu, or a medical emergency. Why had I jumped to poison?

Around us, other people were also shifting in their seats, and murmurs echoed through the auditorium.

"Should we check on him?" Darren asked.

I shrugged. On the one hand, it was probably a good idea. On the other, it's not like Darren the lawyer or me the engineer were qualified to give a medical examination.

Then something strange happened. Mr. Speaker got to the podium and transformed into a regular speaker. He talked in full sentences, and some of the redness left his face.

What was happening?

He stepped away from the podium and immediately stumbled over his words. But when he moved back to the podium, he was again the kind of charismatic, buzzword talker I'd sleep through.

Were his notes on the podium and he couldn't talk without them?

I was about to ask Darren what he thought when a strange almost metallic tearing distracted me. Before I could figure out where the sound came from, there was a crash, and Mr. Speaker lay motionless under a massive stage light that had fallen from the ceiling.

Is it inappropriate to say his speech ended with a bang?

CHAPTER 2

B efore I could really process what happened, a hand clawed into my forearm. It was Darren. His eyes were huge, and he looked like he might puke.

"Darren?"

But he didn't blink. His eyes remained focused on the stage.

"Darren?" I asked again. Then I began trying to remove his hold on my arm. With how tightly he was squeezing, there'd be bruising. My attempt to remove his hand caught Darren's attention, and he finally tore his eyes from the stage. But he dry heaved as soon as he faced me.

I jumped to my feet and tried to get out of the way of any possible vomit—I'm a very supportive friend.

For a moment Darren stared at me with almost vacant eyes, before dropping his head into his hands.

Since throwing up seemed to be off the table for the present time, I sat back down and ended up putting a hand on Darren's back. A man had died. Who knew he'd be so sensitive?

From my spot, it was hard to see what was going on with Mr. Speaker. Most of the people in front of me were standing, blocking my view, and the whole auditorium buzzed with voices. I leaned to one side, but all I could see was a small crowd formed around Mr. Speaker.

From what I could tell, they hadn't found any signs of life. And when emergency responders arrived, instead of loading him onto a stretcher, they took photos of the scene. Safe to assume Mr. Speaker was dead.

Police officers began speaking to event organizers, and the talking around the room had grown so loud I couldn't hear myself think. Darren hadn't moved from his spot staring down at the floor. I patted his shoulder. "It'll be okay."

"Okay?" Darren still wouldn't look up from the floor. "Geoff got pancaked by a stage light. Do you think he'll walk it off?"

I stayed silent—it's a bad idea to argue with an irritated lawyer.

There was a lot more talking between the police and the conference officials before a female detective announced we were supposed to go to the terrace, where the police would take our statements. The auditorium had mostly emptied when I tapped Darren's shoulder. "Terrace," I said.

"I heard," Darren said. Then he stood and stormed off.

All right. Not to be insensitive about what's-his-face getting hit with an ancient stage light, but Darren was really taking this hard. And, technically, we didn't know for sure if he was dead...It's not like we'd been officially notified.

Momentarily forgetting that Britt might be upset with me, I texted: *Help.*

Britt and Juniper were supposed to come back for what had originally been scheduled as a drink and mingle on the terrace. Though now with it turning into police interviews, there wouldn't be alcohol. Plus, Britt and Juniper might not be let in.

Hopefully Britt could spout some paramedic mumbo jumbo or Juniper could bat her eyes and they'd make it to the terrace. Someone needed to check on Darren, and I clearly wasn't qualified.

I checked the time. Britt and Juniper weren't scheduled back for another ninety minutes. Would they tear themselves away from seaweed scrubs and mud baths to give me a hand? Darren could use a friend with more emotional awareness—if *emotional awareness* is even a thing.

When I got to the terrace, I spotted Darren sitting alone at one of those tall barstool tables. As far as I know, he's single and works out enough that he has an impressive upper body. Plus, his face isn't exactly atrocious, and he's usually outgoing...In other words, he was giving some serious *I hate everything* vibes to have absolutely no one attempt a conversation.

I was debating whether I should join him at his table when Rick appeared at my side.

"I hope that wasn't too upsetting for you," he said.

"Umm..."

Was my boss serious?

A quick scan of the area showed many people with gray complexions or red eyes. I had to be one of the least traumatized people in the room. It's not that I'm a terrible person. I've just seen an abnormal number of dead bodies in the past year.

"Anyway," Rick said—clearly not *too* concerned about my mental health, "there's a VIP breakfast tomorrow at six a.m. You have to be there. Details are in the pamphlet from your welcome bag."

"Six in the morning?!"

"The CEO's a morning person. What can you do?" With that, Rick left to bug someone else.

I watched him go, processing what he'd said. I was supposed to be showered, shaved, and dressed all before six? In general I'm more of an early bird than a night owl. Still, I'm not fully dressed for the day by six—especially on work trips. And I'd need to drink a lot of coffee to keep myself from saying something rude.

"There you are," Juniper called, making her way toward me with Britt right behind her.

I don't know what it is about my sister, but her moving through the crowd was like a sudden burst of sunshine for everyone around her. People she walked past relaxed, wrinkles disappeared from foreheads, and a couple of people smiled.

When Juniper got to me, she bent close and asked conspiratorially, "What have you gotten yourself into? When you said you needed help, you could have mentioned the police guard."

I shrugged. "I knew the two of you would figure something out."

"Oh, Juniper definitely did," Britt said, giving my cheek a quick peck. "When the officer said we couldn't go in, her lip started trembling and her eyes were full of tears. It was...impressive."

"What did you say?" I asked.

"You know." Juniper began blinking back tears, and her bottom lip trembled. "'My brother's out there. I'm worried sick about him.'"

"You were *worried sick* about me?"

Juniper tossed her hair. "Well...not exactly."

I raised an eyebrow. "I don't know, that sounds pretty manipulative."

"It worked, didn't it?" Juniper asked.

"What's with the police?" Britt asked, abruptly changing the subject.

Okay.

Juniper and I shared a look. That comment was a clear enough indicator Britt was upset—or maybe she'd spent too much time with people carrying Jacobs DNA.

"Holt." Juniper gave my arm a shake.

Turns out I'd been staring blank-faced at Brittany—not at all creepy.

"Umm, yeah…" Clearing my throat, I tried again. "Darren woke me up during the speech because the speaker was bombing. It was so bad we wondered if he was having a medical emergency. Then, somehow, he was all right and giving a regular speech when a stage light crushed him."

Britt winced, but Juniper sat melodramatically on a barstool beside Darren and asked, "Do we suspect foul play?"

That got a noticeable reaction from Darren. For a moment his eyes flashed with emotion.

"I don't know." I sat next to Juniper. "It was probably foul play. Still, what are the chances a killer would actually get someone to stand in the exact spot where they'd booby-trapped a stage light?"

"That is unlikely," Brittany said, more to herself than to us.

I frowned. Something was wrong with her.

"How was the spa?" I tried.

"Amazing!" Juniper answered for both of them. "Not as good as the place Jude and I went to in Portugal, but still really good."

"Britt?" I asked, hoping this time Juniper would stay silent.

"Don't get me wrong. I love a good foot soak," Brittany said. "But"—her mouth twitched—"I'd also like to hike a few trails while I'm in Arizona, and Juniper's opposed."

Juniper raised her manicured hands up, suddenly defensive. "What's the point of perfecting your feet in a spa if the next day you're just going to wreck it with a bunch of blisters and calluses?"

"And possible toe rot," I added, though I'm not entirely sure what toe rot is.

Brittany nodded at my joke, yet her face had a far-off look.

"Hey," I said, reaching for her hand. "I'd love to go on a hike with you."

Darren surprised us all by snorting. "What Holt wants is to escape Rick walking him around like a show dog."

I grinned. "Added bonus." For Britt's sake I tried to hide how accurate Darren's comment was. "Come on." I tugged Britt closer to me. "Everyone knows how much I love hiking."

That was Juniper's turn to snort.

Britt said, "You know..." before trailing off. There was a sparkle in her eyes, but she wouldn't look at me.

Why was she so hard to read today?

"My brother, Paul, and I try to go on at least one backpacking trip a year. I didn't know if you'd want to come along."

"Oh," I said. Since there were literally no other words that were appropriate enough to be said out loud.

A backpacking trip? One of those get lost in the woods with no internet or cell service? No showers and needing to dig a hole when nature called?

Juniper bursting into laughter brought me back to the present. "Look at his face!" she said when she could get air.

I winced. "Britt, I..."

She tucked an invisible strand of hair behind her ear. "It's fine. I get it. Days in the forest aren't your thing."

Darren let out a low whistle.

Not cool, buddy.

It was like a brick wall was being built between Britt and me today. Somehow the bricks kept getting higher and higher.

I ran a hand through my hair. "Look"—*was I really about to do this?*—"if you'll be there, I'll be there."

If I'd secretly hoped that comment would solve all our problems, it didn't.

Britt nodded and said, "Okay," but she was scanning me with her paramedic face. There was a decent chance she hadn't taken my offer seriously.

"Name the date and I'll be there with a backpack."

"Good luck," Darren muttered.

I glared at him. "What's your problem?" I asked, quietly enough that Britt and Juniper could pretend not to hear.

"You saw that light kill Geoff and you're asking me what's wrong?" Darren kept his voice quiet enough for polite society, but there was an intensity that had a couple of heads turning.

"That was...unfortunate, but we don't really know what happened in there."

"We know he died. Isn't that enough?" Darren stood and would have left if the police weren't manning the doors.

"It's important to remember," Britt said in her professionally friendly voice, "that you both experienced something upsetting, and everyone responds differently to stress."

"*Stress?*" Darren turned on Britt. "A stage light that was installed fifty years ago and has hung with no issues for decades suddenly falls on top of someone, and the only word you've got for me is *stress*?"

"Darren!" I said, getting in between the two of them. "Drop it."

I winced.

Drop it? Like that stage light had dropped? Worst choice of words ever.

There was a stunned silence from Darren and Britt, while Juniper gave a nervous giggle.

"Holt." Britt's hand was on my shoulder. "It's all right. Darren, is this something you want to talk about, or should we leave you alone?"

"Really? None of you get it?" Darren gave a harsh laugh. "First off, there's no way that light fell by accident. We're looking at murder." He waited a moment, letting that fact sink in. "Geoff wasn't supposed to be talking this evening. His speech got switched with Holt's."

I understood Darren's point a second before Juniper.

When my sister got it, her eyes went wide and she gasped. "Holt, someone tried to kill you!"

CHAPTER 3

I'm pretty sure all the air left the room, or my body forgot how to process oxygen. At any rate, everything around me momentarily grayed.

Why would someone want me dead? I'm not saying I'm Mr. Popularity, but I tip well and don't yell at service workers. Sure, that's not exactly a résumé for sainthood, but what have I done to deserve death?

"No," I said, when my brain could formulate words.

Funny thing was, I was no longer standing but was sitting on one of the tall chairs. Brittany's face was inches away from me, while Darren and Juniper hovered on either side.

For half a second it was like I was transported to the stage, giving my speech in front of a crowded auditorium. The moment was so real, I looked up at the sky to double check there wasn't a second stage light waiting to smash me.

"Gargoyles," Britt said.

"Uhh..." I refocused on Britt. "What?"

"Gargoyles. If I were to die by something falling on me, I'd like it to be a stone gargoyle from a Gothic castle."

"Makes sense," I said, resting my head in my hands.

There may have been a lull in the conversation, but to be honest, I wasn't *fully present in the moment.*

"Meteor," Juniper said. "Imagine dying by a shooting star?"

I didn't respond, though it sounded like the others did.

When Darren said he wanted the item falling on him to be a pepperoni pizza that had picked up a fatal amount of force, I caught on.

Sitting up, I said, "I'm not in shock."

"Of course you're not," Britt said, but it was her practiced will-say-anything-to-soothe-the-patient voice.

"Darren, you know I'm fine."

"Sure you are."

"Juniper?"

All she did was shrug.

Finding out someone wanted me dead had been a surprise, and I may have had a *slight* blackout. Still, they didn't need to act all weird.

I glanced toward the exit. The police weren't exactly rushing interviews. Who knew how long I'd be trapped on the terrace with a potential killer.

"What I don't get"—Brittany moved a chair to sit right beside me—"is how you could plan murder by stage light?"

"There could have been someone on the catwalk," Juniper suggested.

Darren shook his head. "If someone was standing on the catwalk, waiting to drop the light, they'd know Holt wasn't giving the speech."

Darren had a good point. I sat up. "The possibility someone wanted what's-his-face dead should be considered."

When Darren opened his mouth to answer, Britt gave a pointed cough and my friend stayed silent.

"Our theories are," Juniper said, tapping away at her phone, "either someone hates Holt so much that they choreographed an onstage murder. They weren't able to stop their plan, which meant Geoff was killed."

Britt coughed again, but Juniper ignored her.

"Or," Juniper said, "Geoff was always the intended victim."

"Either way, it's a pretty complicated way to kill someone," I said.

At that moment, a group of women in their forties who'd been chatting nearby gave me dirty looks and moved farther away. Apparently discussing murder isn't for polite society.

I was tempted to wave my badge and say, *Don't worry. I'm Holt Jacobs, the famous engineer who works for BECKS.*

"Here it is," Juniper said a little too loud given the setting. Realizing her mistake, she waved us close. "Darren mentioned the showcases get recorded. We can go over the footage and figure out what happened."

After tapping a few more keys, Juniper frowned. "Holt, I put in your work email. Now all I need is your conference password."

All eyes turned to me. Heat filled my cheeks. "Here," I said. "I'll type it in."

Smelling blood in the water, Juniper shook her head. "Nice try. Just tell us."

Juniper and I began a stare-off. It didn't take long to decide this wasn't a hill worth dying on. If I didn't tell my sister now, she'd just keep hounding me till she got her answer.

For the record, I know sharing passwords is a security risk, but this site wasn't unlocking state secrets. So, lowering my voice to make sure no one besides my group heard, I said, "Uppercase *B*, lowercase *r*, the number *one*, two lowercase *t*'s, and an exclamation point."

"*Br1tt!*" Juniper's mouth hung half-open.

Darren whistled.

"Holt?" One of Britt's arms wrapped around me.

I tried not to squirm under all the attention.

"You've got it worse than I thought," Darren said.

I sent him my coldest glare, but he wasn't bothered.

"And we're in," Juniper said as the site unlocked.

Brittany and I crowded around Juniper's phone and began watching the recording. Juniper skipped forward to the last couple of minutes. "*We'd like to warn our viewers some of what we're about to show is highly graphic and potentially disturbing,*" Juniper recited in a fake newscaster voice.

"Guess why I'm not watching," Darren said.

Brittany moved her face so close to the phone, the screen was barely an inch away. "You're right. Geoff really doesn't look good."

"Wait for it," Darren said. His eyes were closed, but he could hear the audio.

The change happened a few seconds later. Mr. Speaker reached the podium, and the tension left his face while his shoulders relaxed.

"Do you see that!" I asked, bringing my face right next to Brittany's.

"See what?" Britt asked, turning toward me—our lips were only millimeters apart.

"Don't kiss in front of my phone." And Juniper shoved me away.

I was tempted to kiss Brittany just to annoy Juniper. I didn't. Brittany wouldn't appreciate being a pawn in sibling rivalries.

"Holt?" Britt asked. "What did you notice?"

And Juniper asked, "See what?"

Oh, right.

I'd been so distracted by Britt's face, it took a moment to remember. "Check out his metal water bottle on the podium. The reflection from a light keeps flashing on it."

Juniper zoomed the entire video until just the water bottle was in the frame. She said, "That's almost like...Morse code."

I surprised myself by laughing. "Since when do you know Morse code?"

Juniper rolled her eyes. "I'm not saying it is Morse code. I'm saying all those random flashes of light could be Morse code."

"Morse code," Darren mumbled as he typed into his phone.

"What are you doing?" I asked.

"Keeping track of all the details. Guess how I keep all the facts straight in court."

I shook my head. "I'm pretty sure Morse code won't be a solution to any twenty-first-century crimes."

Darren shrugged as he locked his phone. "We'll see."

"At least someone believes me," Juniper said, shooting me a challenging stare.

"Morse code or not"—Britt sounded like a babysitter trying to break up a squabble—"what's the significance of the flashing light?"

"Hold on." During the whole Morse code debate, I'd set up the replay on my phone and was skipping through with the sound turned off.

"There," I said. "Go to around the nine-minute mark."

Juniper began tapping her screen, while Brittany bent by my phone to see my discovery. This time, with her closeness and scent wafting over me, I did kiss her. But it wasn't to get back at Juniper. My motives were pure. I just wanted to kiss my girlfriend.

"I see it," Juniper said.

"See what?" Brittany asked, being the one to leave the kiss.

"Here." I pressed play.

No doubt against his better judgment, Darren had moved his chair to watch from my other side.

Behind Geoff, barely visible on the scuffed-up stage, was reflected light. It was hard to tell for sure, but it appeared to be the flickering of a dying fluorescent.

"I found another one," Juniper said. "Look at the base of the podium."

She was right. Only this reflecting had the light flashing at a steady rhythm, almost like a strobe light.

"No wonder he had trouble talking," I said.

Darren smirked and began typing notes into his phone.

"What did you say?" I reached for the phone.

"I just wrote 'Holt thinks I'm right.'"

"About what?"

"You being the intended target."

"Uh, I said no such thing."

Darren leaned forward. "Not to pull the whole *I'm a lawyer* card, but yeah, you did."

"No, he didn't," Britt said, unafraid to challenge Darren's lawyerly expertise.

"I'm with Darren on this one," Juniper said. When I raised an eyebrow, she tossed her hair. "What? He didn't laugh me out of the room for suggesting Morse code."

"All right," I said, deciding to play along. "Juniper, describe in your own words how I said anything to agree with Darren's hypothesis that someone wanted me dead."

Juniper said, "That's easy..." But she didn't say anything else.

Britt surprised us by commenting, "We're waiting."

I caught movement in my periphery and turned in time to see Darren mouthing words and giving strange hand signals.

I shook my head. "If you need to cheat to win, it's not a real victory."

Funny thing was, even with Darren's hints, Juniper couldn't answer my question. After waiting a few more seconds, I said, "And just like that, you're out of time."

"Whatever," Juniper said. "How am I supposed to know what"—she duplicated Darren's hand signals—"that means?"

"Your only excuse is Darren wasn't able to help you cheat?" I asked. "I thought you agreed with him." Juniper flushed, and I had a quick jolt as I realized I may have bested my sister. I needed to remember this moment.

Darren shook his head. "What Juniper meant to say was you acknowledged how difficult it would be to give a speech with a lot of different lights flashing at you in different intervals."

"Uh-huh," I said, suspecting I was walking into a trap.

"Well, call me paranoid, but I don't think all those lights suddenly spasming at different frequencies was a coincidence."

I nodded. "I would agree with that, but that doesn't explain why I'm the target."

Juniper laughed, and then her mouth momentarily hung open. "He really doesn't get it?"

"Get what?" I sounded cranky.

Darren tilted his head from side to side. "It would be fairly easy for even someone you barely knew to discover you would find all those lights going off distracting."

"So? Most people would find it distracting."

"He has a point," Brittany added.

"Come on," Darren said. "Holt was scheduled to give the first showcase."

"Well," Britt said, almost apologetically, "if everyone knew the schedule...it would be an easy way to throw Holt off his game."

I shook my head. "I'm not convinced."

"Whatever," Darren said. "Just keep out of abandoned stairwells, and stay in public areas."

"Careful," I said, wishing everyone would stop being so serious on my behalf. "Keep talking like that and I'll think you'd miss me if I was murdered."

Turns out making a joke about someone wanting me dead was in poor taste. No one answered, and an awkward silence stretched on for so long that it stopped being awkward. One by one we each unlocked our phones and began scrolling through feeds or playing level forty-seven in some game.

It was actually turning into a decent way to spend half an hour, but my boss had to ruin it when he reappeared with two execs behind him—Rick was behaving worse than my mom on vacation.

Mom always had a packed schedule of *fun* activities, but at least she didn't expect me to glad-hand strangers.

"Good, you're here," Rick said like the police weren't keeping us all on the terrace. "I was speaking with Sasha Redding and Drew MacIntire about your big discovery, and though I assured them you'd be at breakfast tomorrow, they insisted on meeting you now." The way Rick spoke, it was like he was the master of ceremonies at a circus.

Darren cleared his throat loudly. I twisted my head to see Darren standing up with his shirt smoothed down. I was still sitting.

After setting my phone on the table, I stood and extended my hand with a smile that was more polite than friendly. "Holt Jacobs."

"We know," Male Exec said in a way that made it sound like I was famous.

"Did inspiration strike while you were showering?" Female Exec asked. She turned to her companion. "I swear all the genius types get ideas in the shower."

Apparently this was when I was supposed to answer. Problem was, I was still stuck on an executive asking about what I did in the shower.

When I didn't answer, Rick did on my behalf. "While I'm sure Holt will go into more detail tomorrow"—he shot me a *get your act together* glare—"I can say that what he figured out was more the conclusion to years of hard work than of one lightbulb moment."

"Magnificent," Male Exec said.

"Truly incredible," Female Exec said. "Thanks to your streamlined production process, we're able to close our manufacturing plant in South Dakota."

"Right," I said, and felt another disapproving look from Rick. What did he want from me? I knew about the streamlined production process. That was kind of the whole point. Plus, shutting down the plant in South Dakota was a major reason for the number of zeros in my bonus.

I did my best to keep up with the conversation, but Rick should have known from all the years he'd been my boss that I lacked the desire and charisma to be a golden boy.

When they finally left, it felt like they'd been there for two hours. I sat down and grabbed my phone.

"Um, Darren, would you help me get some water?" Juniper asked. Apparently my sister was worried her *Holt, you need to fix this* tone was too subtle for me to notice. Or that's the best reason I can think of for Juniper swatting the back of my head as she walked past.

I put my phone away and tried to catch Britt's eye, but that proved impossible since she was staring down at the floor. For a moment I considered chasing after Juniper and having her explain what I'd done.

"Sorry for not introducing you to...Rick's friends."

"It's okay," Brittany said, but she wouldn't look at me.

Had I done something now, or did this have to do with why she'd been upset in the hotel lobby?

"I love you," I tried.

Instead of saying it back or even smiling, Britt said, "I know."

I know? Brittany was saying *I know you love me?* Something was very wrong.

Across the terrace, Juniper and Darren were watching. I tried to send an SOS signal, but Darren shook his head and Juniper made a shooing motion with her hands. I had to figure this out by myself.

Since I didn't know what I'd done, I decided to be honest. "If I messed up, please tell me."

Britt's eyes rushed to meet mine, and then she looked to where Juniper and Darren were watching. Instead of answering my question, Brittany asked, "Did Juniper put you up to this?"

Heat filled my face, but I decided Britt deserved the truth. "Sort of," I admitted.

Brittany nodded, her face blank, and it was one of those frustrating times when I had no idea what was going on in her head.

"Britt?"

And again she wouldn't look at me.

I waited a very long time for her to answer, but all I got was silence. Just when I'd given up on her answering, she said, "This isn't a conversation we should have surrounded by your colleagues."

"Are you dumping me?!"

Okay, so maybe I'd jumped to a panicked conclusion. In hindsight I shouldn't have yelled *Are you dumping me?* in a place full of bored colleagues. But what I *should have done* and what I *did do* are two wildly different things.

For a moment the entire terrace full of people was staring at us, and from the way Juniper and Darren rushed closer, they'd definitely heard my outburst from across the terrace.

"Holt..."

I'd never seen Britt's face that pink. It would have been amusing if I weren't worried about what she was going to say. I guess that's the one silver lining. I was too fixated on Britt to be embarrassed about having everyone's attention.

Brittany closed her eyes and began taking long and slow breaths. It was torture to sit through, but Britt couldn't function if she wasn't in control of herself. I had to wait.

The longer Britt breathed, the more aware I was of all the people side-eyeing us. My neck tingled from all the attention. I fiddled with my collar. Finally, I bowed my head into my hands. At least I could ignore everyone around me.

"No."

The voice startled me, and my head snapped up.

"Did you say that?" I asked Britt.

She nodded. Her face was still pink, but the color was fading.

"No?" I repeated, not quite sure what that meant.

"No. I wasn't breaking up with you."

What I hadn't realized was my entire body had clenched up waiting for the worst. I actually got dizzy when my muscles relaxed all at once.

"Okay" was all I could say.

Juniper reappeared at our table. "What happened? What did you say?"

I raised an eyebrow. It was Juniper's fault I'd publicly humiliated myself, and now she wanted to know all the dirt?

"What did *you* say?" And Brittany pinned Juniper with a look that had my sister taking a step back. Neither Britt nor I said anything else, and Juniper ended up leaving, mumbling something about getting more water.

Britt's mouth rose in the ghost of a smile, but there was no sparkle in her eyes.

"We'll talk later?" I asked. It was a relief knowing she wanted to keep seeing me. Still, I hated having a mysterious problem hanging over my head.

Britt analyzed me for a moment. She must have seen desperation, because she finally said, "I didn't realize until today you've been keeping secrets from me."

CHAPTER 4

*W*hat? *Keeping secrets? Me?*

What secrets did I have to keep? I told Britt everything. Even my weird dream where I'd been an astronaut trapped in my space suit.

I must've looked as clueless as I felt, because Brittany squinted at me like she couldn't believe I didn't get it.

I shrugged. "Sorry."

"Oh, Holt..." And Brittany almost rolled her eyes. "I'm talking about how you became an overnight rockstar at your job and didn't mention the promotion, the bonus, the bigger office, or being a featured presenter."

Okay, now I was really confused.

"I did tell you."

"No. I would remember."

I frowned. "We talked...at least about most of it."

"The raise?"

"You called me while you were on a break. I was peeling potatoes for that spicy roast and I told you about the raise."

"Well...I guess you sort of did, but you sounded so casual, I thought it was your annual raise."

"Yeah, no."

"What about the bonus?"

That answer was easy. The bonus had earned a special celebration. "We got all dressed up and went to a fancy restaurant. You asked what the special occasion was, and I told you about the bonus."

Britt's mouth hung open before snapping shut. "Maybe. But what about the bigger office?"

That was a tough one. *Hadn't it come up?*

Wait—I snapped my fingers. "I told you the framed picture of us from the fall gala broke when I was moving offices."

"Ha!" Britt said. "You talked about *moving offices*. You didn't say you were getting a *much bigger office*."

"Britt, come on. First off, no way was I getting a *smaller* office. And if I did, you'd definitely hear about it."

Brittany shook her head, not liking that I was winning this. "Well, what about being a featured presenter?"

My jaw ticked. She had to go there. "I never told a soul I was giving a speech."

"Why not?"

I didn't answer immediately. Instead, I ran a hand through my hair. But she might as well know the truth. "Giving a speech is embarrassing."

Amusement flashed through Britt's eyes, and she shook her head.

"What?" The word came out crankier than I intended.

"Sometimes you're unbelievable."

"Umm...thank you?" *Unbelievable* didn't sound like a compliment, but Brittany was no longer upset.

It ended up being a long, dull evening. Since my work had already reserved the terrace, the police let the servers go past with the appetizers and nonalcoholic beverages, and people like Rick tried to encourage networking and mingling. But the thing about a man dying right in front of you is even the extroverts weren't in much of a mood for socializing.

Brittany and Juniper stayed for over an hour, but being around somber people who were mostly engineers wasn't something either one of them had signed up for—plus, Juniper bores easily.

Darren and I had fallen into a companionable silence on our phones when my new assistant walked up. "Holt?"

I looked up from my phone.

Darren was more polite. He straightened in his chair, slipped his phone into a pocket, and greeted her. "Hello, Gabby."

She smiled politely in his direction. Darren has a reputation for being fairly charming around women, yet with Gabby's looks, she was used to men being extra attentive around her.

"Rick wanted me to remind you about the six o'clock breakfast tomorrow."

"How could I forget?" My voice was dry with sarcasm.

"Wonderful." Gabby ignored the tone. She'd worked at BECKS for around a year and a half and was used to my snarkiness. She'd been hired as Rick's assistant, yet with my recent discovery, Rick had begun sharing his assistant with me—I benefited from Gabby overseeing my busier schedule.

"Don't worry about Holt." Darren grinned. "He'll be there."

I raised an eyebrow. Was Darren going to show up at my room and drag me out of bed if I slept through my alarm?

"I'll be there," I said.

Once Gabby left, Darren shook his head. "A six o'clock breakfast is an early start."

I groaned. "Right? I'm barely social after four cups of coffee."

Darren's a supportive enough friend that he laughed at my predicament. "You'll survive."

I slumped in my seat. My vacations never go as planned. Why should work trips be any different?

Just then Darren's name was called by a detective. "Excuse me."

Wait. Why was Darren giving his statement before me? He didn't have an early-morning breakfast. Also, my last name, *Jacobs*, comes up a lot sooner in the alphabet than *Woods*. It wasn't fair.

"We can meet up after your breakfast," Darren offered. "That way we can sit together during the sessions."

"Thanks," I said. "I'll text you when I'm free."

I was sitting by myself, playing on my phone, when the screen lit up with an incoming call from Mom.

"Hello?" I asked.

"What's this about you becoming Tony Robbins?"

I winced. Juniper is in her twenties, didn't that make her too old to be a tattletale?

"It's a fifteen-minute showcase," I said, lowering my voice. (No one I work with should eavesdrop on my private conversation with my mommy.) "Fifteen minutes is barely a speech."

Mom made that extra-special displeased sound in the back of her throat. "Juniper made it sound like it was a big deal."

My laughter wasn't an act. "You're basing what's important off information *Juniper* gave you? She once faked a dognapping."

"Juniper implied there was an *attempted dognapping*."

Mom must've had the phone on speaker because in the background Dad asked, "What's the difference?"

"My point is," Mom said, ignoring Dad, "just because we moved to Australia doesn't mean you shouldn't tell us when something important is happening in your life."

I frowned at the phone. Mom knew me. I've never been an over-sharer.

When I didn't answer, Mom took a deep breath. "I don't want to visit you in Seattle and discover you're married with two kids."

"Mom"—I inhaled deeply—"of course you'd know if I was married with two kids."

"Promise?"

I shook my head. She really wouldn't let this go. "I promise that Juniper would tell you if I was married with two kids."

"Holt!" Whatever else Mom said went unheard because the female detective from the auditorium was calling my name. "Holt Jacobs?"

"Sorry, Mom. I have to go. The police are ready to interview me."

"The police—"

I disconnected the call before Mom finished speaking. If I didn't acknowledge the detective right away, she might interview someone else, and I'd be left waiting indefinitely for my name to be called again.

"Here!" I practically ran to the detective.

She looked me up and down. Since it was unlikely she was blatantly checking me out, I was likely being assessed for potential weapons. It must be a cop thing. The detective resembled a female superhero, nothing but toned muscles. There was no way she found me threatening. I'm in shape, but I'm not intimidating.

"Mr. Jacobs, if you'll follow me."

She led me past the officer manning the exit and down one of the hotel's long hallways before opening a door to a generic office, where the only artwork was a picture of a tumbleweed. We sat in office chairs, and without any further introduction, she told me to share everything that happened since I'd arrived at Camelback Hotel.

I'd meant to ask Darren if he'd share with the police his theory about my shortened life expectancy. Unfortunately, I hadn't asked, and now I was underprepared for the questions the detective might ask.

For some reason, sitting alone in a small office with an attractive detective had me stumbling over my words. I muddled through and finally reached the death of Mr. Speaker.

"All right." The female detective fell silent as she read something on her tablet. "Now, someone from a previous interview was sure the light falling was intentional."

Since she hadn't asked a question, I didn't reply.

"You were there," she tried. "What's your opinion?"

I leaned back in my chair. Sharing with the police how we'd watched the recording of Mr. Speaker's death and spotted lights flashing erratically in the background was too bizarre to tell a stranger.

It's important not to withhold information from the police. But if you throw out wild theories during an introductory chat, they won't take you seriously.

I smoothed my hair back, trying to come up with a diplomatic answer. "Uhh, if it were me...I'd check all the equipment that held the stage light for signs of tampering. Lights don't just fall from the sky."

Wait. Aren't meteors lights? Don't they literally *fall from the sky*?

At least the detective didn't notice. "Who's idea was it to switch your showcase?"

The question took me off guard. How did she know I was originally scheduled to give that speech? Was she actually considering Mr. Speaker's death as suspicious? Or was she checking the right boxes to ensure if Darren followed up, she could guarantee the case had been thoroughly investigated?

"It was my boss Rick's idea."

"I see." She tapped a few times on her tablet. "And how much notice did he give you of the change?"

"Not much," I said, before worrying that answer was too abrupt. "Look, what's the deal here? Are you treating this death as accidental, or was it murder?"

The detective's expression was unreadable as she stared at me. Finally she admitted, "Geoff Hodges's death is currently classified as: *suspicious, pending further investigation.*"

My shoulders relaxed. At least the police would look further into Mr. Speaker's death. But what would I do if the police determined the death was a freak accident?

CHAPTER 5

By the time I was finally released and could ride the elevator up to my room, I was too worn out to enjoy my suite.

I didn't sit down on the couch or make a snack in the kitchen. Instead, I brushed my teeth, set my alarm, and tumbled into bed. I meant to call Brittany and wish her good night. Problem was, the pillows were down feather, and I was out cold the moment my head sank against them.

It was still dark when my blaring alarm cut through a deep sleep.

That moment probably didn't count as a *dark night of the soul*, but momentarily, half-asleep in the middle of the night, I wondered if skipping the CEO's breakfast was a fireable offense. If it was, would getting fired be worth staying in bed a little longer?

When a second alarm went off, I decided to keep the *getting fired* option as a hypothetical question.

I stood still in the shower for a long time, being pelted with hot water. The water pressure was great, and the temperature was just right. The problem was, my brain became alert enough to start thinking. One idea grabbed ahold of me and wouldn't let go.

Had someone tried to kill me?

While I've never been Mr. Popularity, it's not like I go around shoving people in front of city buses or light people's hair on fire.

If my talk with Brittany proved anything, I'm not always aware of the effect I have on other people. Still, wouldn't I be able to tell if someone hated my guts enough to kill me?

Yesterday it had been easier to laugh off Darren's theory that the stage light was meant for me. This morning it felt a little too real.

In the middle of styling my hair, I paused to stare at the bathroom light. It wouldn't be too hard for anyone at the conference to make the lights flicker. With the fluorescent light, all you'd have to do is twist it half a millimeter.

Probably the biggest concern was the amount of thought it took to plan something so elaborate. You'd have to arrange the lights, making sure the one spot free of flickering was also the spot designed to crush someone with the stage light.

It would be so much simpler if this was all an accident.

Thankfully, I can multitask enough that I could consider reasons I might be killed and get ready simultaneously. I put on my conference lanyard and was heading out the door with five minutes to spare when I remembered I didn't actually know where I was going.

It took longer than you'd expect to find my welcome packet—the one downside of having a massive suite. But once I finally dug it out, I saw the CEO's breakfast was happening on the roof.

After making sure I had my phone, wallet, sunglasses, and room key, I left. The door had just clicked shut when I saw I'd neglected to hang the DO NOT DISTURB sign. I had to swipe back into the room to grab the card and place it on the door handle.

Maybe this is paranoid behavior, but I prefer being the only person in my room. If that means I occasionally reuse towels, so be it.

It was 5:59 a.m. when the elevator door opened on the top floor. I was cutting it a little close, but I was showing up on time, and as a bonus, I was wearing clothes.

There was a glass door leading outside with printed lettering proclaiming THE ROOF. I was in the right place. I knew I was in the right place. But the problem was the door was locked and no one was there. Not good.

I fought the urge to run a hand through my hair since it was already perfect, and instead, I began pacing between the elevator and the glass door. Sure, I was pretty tired when I read the schedule, but I distinctly remember THE ROOF, and I was right by the entrance to THE ROOF.

How had it come to this? My only option was something I do only as a last resort—I had to make a phone call.

I called Rick. The phone rang for so long, I was expecting his voicemail. Instead, the line clicked and I got a croaky "Hello?"

"Are you sleeping?"

"Um...What...? Who...? What time is it?"

"It's six, and I'm trying to get to the roof for the mandatory breakfast and no one's here."

"Breakfast?" Rick said more words after that, but since he was yawning simultaneously, I didn't get the meaning.

"What was that?" I asked.

"It got"—heavy sigh—"postponed to tomorr...Gabby was..." Then snoring.

I swear the man couldn't stay awake long enough to tell me I'd gotten out of bed for no reason. I began running through a list of reasons Rick was a bad boss and a horrible human being. Making me get out of bed for no reason felt like such gross negligence, it should be illegal—though I doubt the police would bother with an arrest.

There was a missed call from Mom, along with an accompanying text that said: *Why are you talking to the police?*

They were from last night, sometime after I'd fallen into bed. Due to the time difference between Phoenix and Australia, I was safe to reply without Mom calling me back immediately.

Holt: *Relax. I wasn't arrested.*

I kept out the bit about the possible threat to my life. If Mom got too worried, she'd jump a plane to Phoenix. However bad ENGINEERS OF THE FUTURE IN THE PRESENT was, it would be much worse with Mom hovering over my shoulder.

I pushed the elevator button harder than necessary. This day was off to a rocky start. Since I needed to tell someone and knew it was too early for Brittany or Juniper to be up, I texted Darren: *Work out?*

He replied within seconds: *I'm already dressed.*

Holt: *I'm not. Meet at my room?*

Then Darren sent the always classy thumbs-up emoji.

My progress was delayed when the elevator stopped two floors before mine, and a hotel worker in a navy uniform and matching hat brought in an empty room service cart. One of the cart's wheels was jammed, and it was a surprisingly complex process to get it onto the elevator.

To further complicate matters, when we stopped on the twentieth floor, I was wedged into the back corner. I had to make a climbing leap over the cart to escape. The hotel employee was laughing at my antics as the doors closed.

Whatever. Being laughed at didn't compare to the breakfast debacle.

The delay meant Darren was exiting his elevator coming up just as I was leaving mine going down.

He whistled. "Either that was a short breakfast, or those are some fancy workout clothes."

Suddenly I regretted texting Darren.

I frowned and said, "I don't want to talk about it."

I began walking to my room. Darren caught up right as I turned the corner to get to my suite. Or what should have been my suite. It was a long hallway, but the door I was walking to had a hotel worker in a navy uniform exiting...and I'd hung a DO NOT DISTURB sign.

I froze. "Wasn't my room next to the stairwell?"

Suddenly Darren had grabbed my arm and was dragging me back around the corner. "Did you order room service?" he asked so quietly I barely heard.

I shook my head.

We peered around the corner and watched the retreating figure disappear into the stairwell.

"Do you recognize them?" Darren asked.

I glared at Darren. He could see for himself how far away they'd been.

"How would I? But we need to find out." And I began running down the hallway, knowing Darren would follow.

I'd opened the door to the stairs and was listening for any echoes of movement on the landing when Darren caught up.

"Anything?" he asked.

I shook my head. "I'll go down. You go up."

Before Darren could argue about it being dangerous to split up, I was already charging downstairs. I'd gone down one flight when the click of a door somewhere beneath me had me launching myself even faster.

Two flights down, I left the stairs and ran into the hallway. But I didn't spot anyone in hotel uniforms—all I saw was a middle-aged shirtless man with a towel around his waist.

Had the shirtless man taken the stairs?

I jogged through all the turns in the hallway but didn't find any hotel employees. I also didn't find an abandoned hotel uniform—that sort of thing is always happening in Mission: Impossible movies.

Once I thought I heard Rick's voice, but when I rounded the corner, no one was there. I could have misheard, or Rick might be staying on this floor.

When I got back to my floor, Darren was waiting by my door.

"Anything?" Darren asked.

"I got a shirtless man wrapped in a towel. You?"

"A crying baby."

An uneasy silence began as we both eyed my door suspiciously.

"Let's go check in the lobby and see if they sent someone up," Darren said.

"At six in the morning with a Do Not Disturb sign?"

Darren shrugged. "Might as well check before we call the police."

The police?

"You still think someone is trying to kill me?"

"Absolutely."

Hopefully Darren was wrong, but this newest incident was making that possibility harder to ignore. And it's not like I wanted to go into my room without an explanation from the hotel or an armed escort.

At the front desk, I momentarily froze. How was I supposed to ask, *Did you send someone to my room, or is someone trying to kill me?*

Before I came up with an appropriate question, Darren asked, "Can you check if any staff were sent to room 2071?"

"And what is this in reference to?" The hotel worker's face remained neutrally pleasant, but I got the sense he'd need a pretty good reason to divulge any personal information.

I had to be charming. "Morning," I said with a half smile. "My name's Holt Jacobs. I'm here for the engineering seminar, and I'm staying in room 2071."

"I see," said the hotel clerk, giving me nothing but professional politeness.

"Anyway, this morning when I was coming back to my room, someone dressed in a hotel uniform was leaving my room. It seemed...suspicious."

Partway through my speech, the clerk began typing on the keyboard. When he looked up, some of the manufactured pleasantness was gone. "According to our system, a housekeeping key card was used to enter your room." He swallowed. "Uh, they don't start cleaning until ten."

"Police it is," Darren said with his phone already unlocked.

Darren gave a brief explanation, then was put on hold and transferred, before going into more detail with a new officer, since today's trespassing might be linked to last night's death. When he hung up, Darren told me, "The detective will call when she gets here."

I nodded.

"Come on," Darren said. "Let's get some breakfast. We'll have to skip the workout."

I followed Darren without an argument. I was running out of excuses for why someone *wasn't* trying to kill me, and that bummed me out.

If I worked off the hypothesis someone wanted me dead, everyone I knew was a suspect.

I eyed Darren, momentarily worried he'd poison my coffee.

Apparently he caught the look, because Darren asked, "What? You want to drink out of the same glass to make sure I don't sweeten your coffee with arsenic?"

"Well…" I said, embarrassed he'd read my mind. "You came up with that example pretty fast."

Darren shrugged, not at all bothered by the accusation. "Can I help it if I'm suspicious?"

CHAPTER 6

"Where am I on your list of suspects?" Darren asked after we finished eating.

"Well, assuming I don't drop dead in the next five minutes, I'd say you're pretty low on the list."

Darren winked. "Good to know."

We cleaned up our empty dishes, and Darren began heading toward the lobby.

For half a second I wondered if he was luring me into a false sense of security for a sneak attack. Then a new idea hit.

Darren realized I hadn't followed and walked back to the dining area. "You know I'm messing with you," he said.

"Uh, yeah. Sure." I squinted at nothing in particular. "But why now?"

"Excuse me?" Darren twisted his head like he expected to see what I was staring at.

"Why try to kill me in Phoenix? Wouldn't it be easier to murder me in Seattle when I'm on my regular schedule?"

"Okay." Darren's brows creased as he thought it through. "There are two main options. One, the killer wants you dead but either doesn't live in Seattle or doesn't have ready access to your life."

For a moment I started to relax. If that was true, all I'd need to do was survive two more nights in Phoenix and I'd be safe when I got back home.

But Darren had a second option, and it was less comforting. "Or the killer is someone who knows you so well they'd be an obvious suspect. They waited until the conference to create a wider pool of suspects."

"Well, that keeps you on the list," I said, trying to sound like it was a joke.

"I guess it does." Darren played along with the lighthearted banter, but his eyes remained serious. No matter what we said, neither one of us was taking the threat on my life lightly.

"Let's go," Darren said, since I was still standing in the middle of the hotel dining room. "The police should be here soon."

When the superhero detective from last night strode in, she immediately spotted me, but then her attention landed on Darren. "It's you." She gasped, and half covered her mouth like she wanted to take the words back.

Instead of winking and saying something flirtatious, Darren frowned. "Why's a detective responding to a disturbance call?"

The detective raised her eyebrows, not expecting to have her appearance challenged. "Holt's name is on a list, and I was notified by dispatch."

Darren's jaw tightened. "Now you agree that someone tried to kill him last night?"

"Not officially. But"—she lowered her voice—"the auditorium lights were tampered with, and the stage light that crushed Mr. Hodges was missing screws. His death is an ongoing investigation."

"Good," Darren muttered.

I don't know what happened during Darren's police interview last night, but today's conversation felt like the continuation of an argument.

It was very uncomfortable. I decided to break up the tension with a question. "Is now a good time to check my room?"

"Of course. It's why I'm here." The detective shot a glance at Darren before leading the way to the elevators.

Once we reached my room, Darren and I stayed in the hallway as the detective used my key card to unlock the door. She drew her gun and disappeared inside.

I didn't actually ask Darren why he'd been combative with the detective—I looked from him to the door and cleared my throat.

Darren leaned against the wall, pretending to be relaxed. "I may have questioned her competency last night after I used the word *murder* and she said Geoff's death hadn't been ruled a homicide."

I barked out a laugh. No wonder there was tension. Darren must've presented his argument like a lawyer should, but I couldn't blame the detective for not taking the stranger spouting conspiracy theories seriously.

"It's your life I'm worried about," Darren said. "You could be a little more concerned."

"If being *more concerned* means I'm rude to the police detective who's investigating the case, I'm gonna pass."

Darren grunted, and we fell silent.

Time passed, and the detective was still in my suite. I began to pace around Darren. "What if there's nothing wrong?" First Darren had implied she was dumb. Now I may have brought her to the hotel on a wild-goose chase.

Darren shrugged.

"Was that person leaving my room?"

"Yeah," Darren said. "Aren't you sure?"

"Pretty sure," I said, leaning against the wall. Something about the police actually investigating the room made me worried I was the boy who cried wolf.

"Was Detective Bunny the one who interviewed you last night?" Darren asked.

Hold on. What had Darren called her?

This detective didn't resemble a cute baby bunny. Our detective was...What was the right way to describe her? She was definitely attractive, in a super-fit, could-be-a-stunt-double-in-superhero-movies sort of way. I'm secure enough in my manhood to admit it: she terrified me.

"You called *that* woman Detective *Bunny*?"

"So?"

It's not that I would judge someone for giving people little nicknames. Still, wasn't *Detective Bunny* kind of offensive?

"Would you relax?" Darren said. "That's her name."

"Her name is *Bunny*?" I wasn't buying it. "You didn't make up *Detective Bunny*?"

Darren shook his head.

"Because *Detective Bunny* is eerily similar to *Badge Bunny*."

"Holt." Darren's eyes were huge as he pretended to be offended. "That woman in there is risking her life to protect us. I would never disrespect that."

"Right, you'll just imply she's incompetent."

"I was merely stating my opinion of how the case was being handled."

"Sure," I said, then fell silent. I tried to let the name go. I kept my mouth shut for at least twelve seconds, but it was too absurd. "Her parents are the *Bunnys*? Mr. and Mrs. Bunny?"

Half of Darren's mouth crooked up. "I don't know if her parents are still together."

Huh. It seemed like he was actually telling the truth, yet it was hard to believe.

The door swung open, and the lady in question stepped out.

There, sewn on for all the world to see, was a patch with our detective's last name. It was indeed *Bunny*. I would have noticed the patch on her uniform without Darren giving a fake cough. The fact he thought he needed to was insulting.

Detective Bunny's face was more serious than when she'd entered the hotel. "Mr. Jacobs, it appears your room's been vandalized."

"Oh" is all I said. While I definitely felt violated, I was surprised by the relief it wasn't in my head.

"What did they do?" Darren asked, straightening his workout tank like he was about to give a closing argument.

Detective Bunny opened the door wider. "It's in the bedroom."

We walked through the kitchen and living room areas, all eerily undisturbed. I froze when I got to the bedroom door, and Darren walked into me. All eight of my feather-down pillows had been cut open, and the entire room was an inch or two deep with tiny feathers.

When I could speak, I asked, "Will I need to pay for the damages?"

Behind me, Darren half gagged in an attempt to stifle his laughter.

Detective Bunny remained serious. "We'll talk to the manager. Usually this sort of thing is covered by insurance."

This sort of thing? How often did vandals tear open pillows in hotel rooms? I've never heard of it happening—granted my social circle is pretty limited.

Detective Bunny asked, "Can you describe the person you saw?"

I shrugged and looked at Darren, who shook his head. I said, "All I saw was the hotel uniform. They were leaving my room just after six."

"Gender?" When all Detective Bunny got was blank stares, she asked more questions. "Hair color? Height? Weight?"

"Umm...average weight?"

"Okay." Detective Bunny frowned down at her tablet. "Our suspect was someone dressed in a Camelback Hotel uniform who was average weight."

"That sounds about right," Darren said.

With how hard Detective Bunny was looking anywhere but at Darren, she had to be fighting the urge to imply he was incompetent in identifying suspects.

"We can go talk to the manager on duty. They'll send someone to clean up the mess and replace your pillows. Then I'll"—she hesitated, looking from her tablet to me to the room full of feathers—"file my report."

At least she had a lot to go off.

"Can he get a new room?" Darren asked.

"We can ask. But"—Detective Bunny hesitated—"the vandal had a master key and was able to track down Holt's current room. It's highly likely they'd be able to find him again."

Darren's face tightened with frustration, but this time he didn't go *full lawyer*.

It was almost time for our first seminar to start. Darren went to change into business clothes while I went to the lobby with Detective Bunny.

Shockingly, the manager couldn't comment on whether or not the person who'd broken into my room was a hotel employee. Apparently *average weight* wasn't enough to go off.

The manager clarified I wouldn't be charged for the pillows. Yet, due to my engineering conference, the hotel was fully booked, and I was unable to switch rooms.

While I was stuck with my room, he assured me the mess would be cleaned up and gave me a gift certificate to stay at the Camelback Hotel for two nights for free...because I make so many trips to Phoenix.

I wasn't invited to join them in tracking down who the key card belonged to, but my guess was one of the staff would be reporting their card missing. At any rate, that card would be deactivated.

I didn't exactly feel safe when I left Detective Bunny and the hotel manager, but what else could they do?

After Darren and I met up and got coffee, we were just in time for the morning session. This was a small-group workshop, team-unity thing. I had to stay awake and contribute from time to time.

When we were released for lunch, Brittany, Juniper, and Chouzie were waiting in the lobby.

For a moment I was jealous. They were on a real vacation, wearing comfortable clothes, while I was dressed for work, trying to come up with a new slogan that *embodied our company's spirit*—what does that even mean?

"You both look relaxed," I said before kissing Britt.

"Next time we'll go to the spa," Darren said.

Before they could say anything, my new assistant appeared. "Excuse me," Gabby said. "Can I steal you for a minute?"

"Sure." I followed Gabby to a quieter spot in the large lobby. "What's going on?"

"Rick sent me." She was too used to his shenanigans to be at all embarrassed about delivering his messages.

"Rick?" I crossed my arms. It was because of him I got up at the crack of dawn for no reason.

"He wanted me to make sure you were all right after this morning's miscommunication."

He sent our shared assistant hoping I wouldn't shoot the messenger?

"Rick said"—Gabby hesitated—"Rick said he told you last night about the postponement."

I opened my mouth, but no sound came out.

No.

He hadn't.

Not having to get up at 5:00 a.m. for a 6:00 a.m. breakfast is absolutely something I would've remembered.

"You can tell him"—my jaw ticked—"you can say I got the message, and if he wants to talk more about the *miscommunication*, he'd better do it in person."

"Understood," Gabby said.

As she was leaving, I remembered to say, "Thanks."

On my way back, I could tell something was wrong. Britt's face was unreadable, while Juniper was staring at me with arms crossed and hip popped, and Darren looked a little guilty.

"You have an assistant?" Juniper asked.

"Um, no...well, sort of."

Juniper's nose wrinkled. "*Sort of?*"

"She's kind of a shared assistant. She's been Rick's assistant for a while, but now she's also helping me." I shot Darren a look that asked, *What did you tell them?* But Darren just winked.

"And why haven't you mentioned your hot young *shared* assistant?" Juniper asked.

"Because it's none of your business." It was the wrong answer. I knew it was the wrong answer right after the words were out of my mouth. Darren's bulging eyes were just the added confirmation I'd messed up.

But I could fix this. Before Juniper came up with her next question or accusation, I said, "Why would I tell you about any of my coworkers?"

"Fine." Juniper tossed her hair. "But you've at least told Brittany about…"

"Gabby," I said. "And no. What's there to tell? *Oh, Britt, my assistant, Gabby, rescheduled my meeting to the afternoon.* Not exactly riveting conversation."

"Holt, she looks like a ballet dancer," Juniper said.

"Didn't she dance at some conservatory?" Darren asked—because he loved making my life more complicated.

"I don't see what my shared assistant's hobbies have to do with what I tell my girlfriend."

"Point is"—Juniper stuck a manicured finger in my face—"you should have told Britt you have a *hot* assistant."

I looked at Brittany. She'd stayed silent the whole time, neither agreeing nor disagreeing with Juniper.

What was I supposed to do?

Luckily, inspiration struck. I began to smirk—I had it. "So, Juniper, you're saying a partner needs to tell their significant other about attractive people they spend time with in the workplace?"

"Uh-huh."

"Does that mean Britt should share all the details about the firemen she sees on a daily basis?"

"Well…"

I'd stumped her.

Finally, all Juniper said was "That's different."

"How?" I asked—managing not to start applauding at my own brilliance.

"Because...it is." Juniper moved her arm like Chouzie was tugging on the leash, though we could all see he was sitting patiently at her feet. "Now, excuse me. Chouzie needs to go out."

I winked. "Sure he does."

Juniper stuck her tongue out as she left.

Real mature.

As soon as Juniper left, Darren pretended to get a phone call, leaving me and Britt alone.

"So, Brittany"—I knew a lot was riding on how she reacted—"I should tell you, I have someone who assists me throughout the day."

Britt nodded, but I couldn't tell if she was amused. "Almost like an assistant?"

I gave a weak grin. "That's one word for it."

Britt tucked an invisible strand of hair behind her ear. "Should I show you some photos of my firemen coworkers?"

"Maybe later." My voice was a low growl, and my chest had swelled. I momentarily forgot I was in a hotel lobby with random colleagues as I closed the distance between us. My head was bent toward Britt, and our lips were about to touch when Britt took a step back. "Did Gabby help you move?"

"Huh?"

"When you got the bigger office, did Gabby help move your stuff?"

"Sure. I guess so."

What was happening? I wanted to be kissing Brittany, not discussing who carried my stapler and paper clips.

"Is it possible"—Brittany lowered her voice—"that Gabby broke the picture of the two of us on purpose?"

I groaned. "You're turning into Juniper."

"And that's a good thing," my sister said, somehow sneaking up behind me. "Has Brittany cracked the case?"

"No," I said, right as Brittany said, "Maybe."

"What's going on?" Darren asked, suddenly reappearing.

"Brittany wants to know if Gabby could have smashed a photo of the two of us when she helped me move offices."

"Interesting," Darren said. His eyes grew distant as he thought that through. "And she'd do this because..." Darren trailed off and tilted his head in my direction.

Britt and Juniper both nodded.

I rolled my eyes. "Hey! Don't be rude. If you're thinking, *It would be horrible to be Holt's assistant. That poor woman wants him dead.* You're all wrong. I'm a delight to work for."

"That's not what we meant," Brittany said.

Juniper was giggling so hard, all she could say was "Oh, Holt."

If the implication wasn't *Holt's a horrible boss*, I didn't understand the inside joke they were sharing.

"They think Gabby's in love with you," Darren said, getting straight to the point.

"Sure," I said—the word coming out as almost a laugh. "Yeah, Gabby is so deeply in love with me, seeing a photo of me with another woman causes such a jealous rage that she had to destroy it." I raised my eyebrows. "Sound about right?"

Britt shrugged. "It's a theory."

CHAPTER 7

I wasn't buying it.

"In this theory, Gabby first intentionally destroyed a picture of me and my girlfriend, then weeks later set up an elaborate murder because she loved me so much she wanted me dead?"

No one answered.

"Not to be rude, but if she wants me that bad, why would she kill me? Wouldn't she go after Britt?"

"Holt!" Juniper's eyes were wide, and she seemed genuinely shocked.

But I'd gotten up at 5:00 a.m. and didn't have the time to walk through a social minefield. "What? You're all allowed to talk about how I'm a walking murder victim, but the second I point out your main suspect would have a more obvious target, I'm a bad person?"

"Yup," Darren said, slapping my back. "Now, are we eating or what?"

I'm not sure what the other restaurant options were at the Camelback Hotel complex, but the one we ended up at had an outdoor patio overlooking a swimming pool and decorative cacti.

Darren filled Juniper and Brittany in on the pillows that were torn to shreds while I tried to figure out whether Gabby was actually in love with me.

Were they basing this suggestion on something?

Maybe body language?

Her attentiveness?

Or was it nothing more than hoping my hot assistant would be out of the picture very soon?

Juniper poked me. "Somebody cut open your pillows and you're still not paying any attention to your surroundings?"

"And?" It's not like I'd missed anything. Everyone was in the exact same places they'd been the last time I'd tuned in—the food hadn't even been delivered. I winked. "Between the three of you, I trust you'd spot anyone slipping cyanide into my water."

When everyone kept staring at me like I was an idiot for not keeping track of who might be approaching with a knife, I added, "Besides, Darren called the police, and Detective Bunny is looking into it."

Brittany choked on her water while Juniper asked, "Who?"

"Detective Bunny."

Juniper asked Darren, "What's her real name?" But Darren was enjoying himself too much to answer.

I raised my right hand. "I swear her uniform said B-U-N-N-Y."

The scar by Britt's eyebrow creased. "Maybe it's pronounced *Bueh-nee*."

"That seems likely," I muttered.

"Did Detective"—Juniper hesitated—"Bunny think the intruder had planned on stabbing you with the knife they used to cut the pillows open?"

I sat back to stare at her. Detective Bunny hadn't suggested that. I hadn't considered they'd broken in to stab me in my sleep.

"I assumed the cut-up pillows meant they were planning on using a pillow to suffocate him," Britt said almost casually.

I looked at Darren. "Any theories you'd like to add?"

"Well"—Darren half smiled—"what I've been wondering is whether the person knew you'd be out of your room. If they knew you'd be gone, maybe the slashed pillows were some sort of warning."

"That would make Rick an obvious suspect," I said. "He knew my schedule."

"Or—and you know I hate to say this—it could also mean Gabby," Juniper said.

I rolled my eyes. Juniper definitely didn't hate suggesting Gabby was a suspect.

"Like, what if Rick told Gabby to inform you about the rescheduled breakfast?" Brittany said, since my sister and my girlfriend wanted my shared assistant to be an obsessed killer.

"Suspects aside," I said, since there was no use arguing that Gabby wasn't trying to kill me. "Using Occam's razor, which is more likely? Someone steals a room card from a housekeeper to make a second attempt at murdering me or for the sole purpose of destroying a few pillows?"

The answer was obvious, and we all knew it.

Someone wanted me dead.

Tension began forming in my temples. I'd accidentally survived a second attempt on my life.

"Or," Brittany said, nodding like she was trying really hard to find a reason Darren's theory would prove correct. "Or, the cut-up pillows were a message. Does any of your work deal with textiles?"

"Or birds," Juniper added.

"Or feathers?" I added dryly. In spite of my growing headache, I was almost grinning. "No. I can't say much of my work deals with textiles, or birds, or feathers."

"Well, now that we've cleared that up"—Juniper was in no mood to spare my feelings—"what motives are there for wanting Holt dead?"

Everyone looked at me like I should know the answer.

"How should I know?" I said. "I don't go around punching people."

"Yes," Juniper said, "But your personality is a bit of an acquired taste."

"And that's a strong enough reason to kill me?"

"Maybe," Juniper said. "Either it's your personality, or you've made a new enemy. Let's go through any changes in your routine."

The food arrived. It all looked great, but I'd kind of lost my appetite. Though I got a forkful of fettuccine, I couldn't actually put the food in my mouth. Setting down the fork, I considered Juniper's question. "I don't know. Not much has changed. I'm at the same apartment, working for the same company."

"Except you got a big promotion," Darren said.

"And a girlfriend," Brittany said. Then she took my fork and made me take a bite. Since I couldn't politely talk with a mouthful of food, the annoyed glare I sent Britt said, *How could I forget my girlfriend?*

"I do like the unrequited love angle," Juniper said. "Assuming it's Gabby—"

I swallowed in time to say, "It's not Gabby."

"Whatever," Juniper said—though I was actually more focused on the food Brittany was trying to get in my mouth than what my sister was saying.

"Since when did we decide Holt has a fleet of women who are secretly in love with him?" Darren asked.

Juniper answered, "Since we found out his secret assistant is a ballet dancer." Her phone lit up on the table. Juniper glanced at the screen, then gave a dangerous smile. "Mom's been texting. She wants to know why you were talking to the police."

I glared at Juniper. "Don't say anything. Because of you, Mom already thinks I'm pursuing a career in public speaking. Don't you dare tell her about the whole"—I lowered my voice—"attempted murder thing."

Juniper pursed her lips together in mock concentration. "I don't know. Mom doesn't like it when I keep secrets from her."

"She'll live," I muttered.

"And"—Darren's eyes glinted dangerously—"you'd better honor Holt's wishes. If he's killed, you'd be racked with guilt over not following his final request."

"Darren!" Britt's mouth hung open, but I'd started laughing.

"That's why I keep a lawyer around," I said. "Let the record show that I, Holt Jacobs, will haunt Juniper in the event of my untimely demise if certain sensitive details are divulged to the defendant's mother."

Juniper wrinkled her nose. "You don't believe in ghosts."

"Eh, I'd figure something out."

"This is a bad argument," Britt said. For a moment I worried Darren and I were being too cavalier, but then I caught the slight tremble as she fought a smile. "Who do you think Juniper's more afraid of? A ghostly apparition of her brother or her mother when she finds out Juniper knew about Holt's death threats?"

Darren raised his hands. "I withdraw my case."

"You're too smart for us," I told Britt.

We were about to kiss when Rick's "There he is," announced his presence loud enough that heads turned from nearby tables. "You don't mind if I steal him away?"

Brittany's back went rigid. "He's eating."

Rick pretended not to hear as he *helped* me out of my chair. "Gabby said she talked to you and you were very understanding about this morning's mix-up."

He took my silence as agreement.

As I started to leave, Darren mouthed, *Don't get murdered,* and accompanied the gesture with a finger slicing across his throat.

Few people are blessed to have such caring friends.

Maybe I should've taken Darren's advice more seriously. I'd been following Rick on autopilot, figuring I was about to meet another bunch of people who acted like I was a thirty-year-old prodigy. Then suddenly I was in a dark hallway that didn't have the same level of upkeep as the rest of the hotel—one might even call it dingy.

I stopped walking and was contemplating turning around when my boss pushed a side door open. "Come on," he said.

I followed. It's amazing what I'll do for a paycheck.

Though I was right behind Rick, I still got tangled in a set of heavy navy curtains hanging from the rafters. When I'd managed to free myself, it was to discover I was just offstage from where Mr. Speaker died.

"Rick...?" I was too confused to bolt. What possible reason could he have for bringing me here?

"Don't tell me you're bothered by Geoff dying here." Rick shook his head like he expected better. "I thought you were used to stuff like that after the vacation you took last May."

Rick didn't know the half of it. My trip to Amelia's Haven made national news, and I'd had to delay my return to work after being injured in pursuit of justice, but that wasn't my only adventure involving dead bodies.

I walked onstage and craned my neck back to get a better view of the lights. Then I remembered I was supposed to be suspicious of anyone

I spent time with since they might try to kill me. I'd turned my back on Rick—practically inviting him to make a sneak attack.

"I don't understand," I said, facing Rick. "Isn't this a crime scene?"

"No." Rick looked around the stage. "Why would it be?"

I tilted my head in the direction of the podium.

"That?" My boss shook his head. "Crime scenes are for when *crimes* occur, not freak accidents."

What?

Even if Detective Bunny had told me privileged information, Rick was smart enough to know that the police hadn't quarantined an entire conference for interviews because the death was *accidental*.

While I get that rigging an elaborate system of lights to force a person to stand in one spot is unlikely, the odds of someone happening to stand where a stage light—that's hung for decades without problems—crashes to the ground...well, let's just say I think your chances are better at winning the lottery twice.

Rick was watching me, and I had no idea what he was thinking. A new fear arose that he was trying to frame me. Had I touched anything? Had I fixed my hair and shed loose strands of DNA-filled hair on a stage that was supposedly *not* a crime scene.

"What was so important I had to skip lunch?" I asked.

"I was going to help you with your speech."

Huh?

"You took me away from lunch with my girlfriend because you wanted to hear my speech?"

Rick ignored the question as he brought a folding chair onstage and sat.

I crossed my arms. "No. Not happening."

"Hmm," Rick said with the unimpressed tone of someone who controls your salary.

"Sorry," I said, moving downstage toward the seats so I could take the main exit. Best to be in groups of people as fast as possible.

"It'll only take fifteen minutes," Rick said, not bothering to get up from his chair.

"Exactly. If I bomb, it'll be over quickly."

"Come on, Holt. It's...it"—Rick stuttered over the word, his face growing red—"it's not to say you don't have your charms. But, well, it's important that you present your best self."

My best self? What was that supposed to mean?

"I'll try to remember to shave." I took the stairs off the stage and exited the theater through the auditorium.

What was happening?

I'd worked for Rick for years and for the most part I liked him as a boss. It was only now when everyone thought I was a genius that he'd become weird and overbearing. I froze in the hallway leading to the lobby next to a decorative cactus as the timing of Mr. Speaker's death hit me.

That was scheduled to be my crowning moment. I was supposed to go up there and explain to our company and our competitors why I was brilliant. Instead, I would have sweated and stumbled over my words, distracted by the flickering lights before experiencing a *tragic accident*.

Darren was right. Choosing to kill me in Arizona meant something. But trying to discredit me in the minutes leading up to my death also held meaning.

Whoever the killer was, they hated me because of my new ideas.

I was still standing by the decorative cactus when Gabby approached. "Have you checked your email?"

Gabby wasn't trying to kill me...but what if she was?

I shook my head, trying to act normal. "Not since last night." With everyone here at Camelback Hotel, there hadn't been much in my inbox. I hadn't bothered checking this morning. Unlocking my phone, I opened the app for my work inbox. "What am I looking for?"

"I don't know."

For the first time, I actually looked at Gabby. Her face was flushed, and her breathing was shallow.

"Gabby?"

She lifted one shoulder—uncharacteristically casual for the former ballet dancer. "Maybe it's a joke."

It didn't take long to find the email that had her worried. Though it's a wonder it made it into my inbox since the sender's address was nothing but a random jumble of letters and numbers.

Below the highlighted banner warning me the sender didn't work for BECKS were three simple words.

HOLT MUST PAY.

My grip on the phone tightened as I reread the words.

"How did you know about this?" I took a step back and checked Gabby for possible weapons.

"I was blind cc'd."

Blind cc'd?

Someone had taken the time to create a dummy email address and not only sent me a threat but cc'd my assistant? Who else was blind cc'd?

"Are you okay?" Darren asked as he strode across the hallway trailed by Britt, Juniper, and Chouzie.

At the same time, from the opposite direction, Rick approached. "What's this about?"

Both Darren and Rick were holding their phones, and if I had to put money on it, I'd bet they were also blind cc'd.

I was trying to come up with a suitably vague answer when my sister blurted, "Someone's trying to kill Holt."

Good one, sis.

Both Gabby and Rick looked at me like I was expected to say something. "Uhh...it's a hypothesis we're considering."

"*Holt must pay* for what?" Rick asked, clearly more concerned I'd committed a crime that could get the company sued.

"That's what I wanted to know." Gabby's already perfect posture grew even more perfect. "It's not like he's embezzling."

"Is someone embezzling?" Rick asked.

"No one's embezzling," I said.

When both Rick and Gabby weren't looking, Juniper nodded and winked like she knew I was a filthy embezzler but the secret was safe with her. If I hadn't been with my boss and my employee, I would have rolled my eyes, but given the circumstances, I didn't respond.

"I've already forwarded this on to IT," Gabby said, doing what all good assistants did and somehow managing to be a step ahead of everyone else. "Should we call the police?"

"Here," Darren said. "I just forwarded it to the detective who was here because of the hotel room."

"What hotel room?" Rick asked.

Seriously, everyone needed to stop talking.

"A problem with the pillows," I said, then walked away with the hope no one would follow.

"Remember Teams for Teamwork starts in fifteen minutes," Gabby called.

I waved a hand but didn't turn back. I couldn't be there as Darren or Juniper detailed the murders of several feather pillows.

I thought I'd not only made a clean getaway but was lucky enough to ride in an empty elevator—like the doors were practically shut when a hand shot through and they reopened.

At least I wasn't at risk of dying alone.

CHAPTER 8

"Brittany," I said, sounding grumpier than I intended.

"Holt." She hesitated outside the elevator.

I tilted my head to the empty spot beside me and tried to grin. "Going up?"

"Sure."

We rode in silence. I was going to my room for the sole reason of getting some quiet—and a morbid curiosity to see whether the thousands of tiny feathers had been removed.

When I carded into my room, Brittany said, "Nice place."

"Except for all the feathers." I led the way to the bedroom but hesitated in the hallway. I'm not proud of this, but Brittany ended up pushing the door open.

"It's clean," she said.

Only then did I walk into the room. But somehow the missing feathers and freshly puffed pillows on the bed creeped me out. I needed to leave. "Come on."

"Um, okay." Britt glanced at the clock, and I knew she was calculating how much time was left before I would be late for Teams for Teamwork.

When I got to the living room, I sat back against the couch, closed my eyes, and let out a breath that I felt like I'd been holding all day. I expected Britt to sit beside me, squeeze my knee, and say something encouraging. Instead, I heard her moving around the kitchen but was too lazy to crack an eye open to find out what she was up to.

"Here."

I was startled out of a doze by Brittany standing in front of me with a travel cup of what had to be coffee.

"You're pretty great," I said before taking a long drink of coffee.

She held out her hand. "Now, come on. You have a seminar to get to."

I groaned. "You're less great."

Brittany took the free hand I wasn't offering and hauled me to my feet. "What's the rush?" I grumbled before drinking more coffee.

"If we don't leave now, Gabby will get you."

Gabby? I couldn't see Britt's face since she was halfway to the door, but there was a tone I didn't like. "Hold on," I said, hurrying to catch up. "There's nothing going on there. You know that, right?"

"Yes," Britt said, but she wouldn't meet my eyes.

"Hey." I bent down, trying to catch her brown eyes. "Ask anyone in my family. You're the only woman I've ever loved."

Britt nodded, but the tension didn't leave her face.

A grin threatened to split my face when I realized what was going on. "Let's go," I said.

"What just happened?" Now Britt had her hand on the door, blocking me from opening it.

I shrugged, knowing it was better not to answer.

"Holt?"

"I just figured something out," I said.

But Britt didn't open the door.

"Uhh..." I tried to think up an excuse, but my stupid grin wouldn't leave. I'd have to tell her the truth. "It seems like you're jealous."

Brittany blinked. "And that's what's got you smiling like the Cheshire cat?"

"Yup."

Brittany shook her head, but she opened the door and started walking to the elevators. "You're unbelievable."

"I love you."

Britt half snorted, but she said, "I love you too."

When the elevator doors opened on the lobby, Gabby stood waiting, clearly about to go up. "Oh." She took a step back and seemed surprised at finding Britt and me together. "Are you ready?"

"You know I'm never ready for these things."

"Great," she said, ignoring the sarcasm. "Let's go."

"Have a good afternoon," I said, giving Britt a quick kiss.

"Be careful," she whispered before Gabby could drag me away.

"The two of you seem all right," Gabby said as we walked to the Sun Room event space that was reserved for programs organized only for BECKS employees.

"Excuse me?"

"Oh"—Gabby flushed—"I heard you yell something about breaking up last night."

Of course she had. What had I been thinking? But more importantly, why was she asking? Was Gabby actually in love with me?

Ugh. Why would Juniper put that idea in my head? Then again, why was Gabby asking about my girlfriend? It's not like we had a working relationship that involved chatting about our significant others.

Gabby successfully got me to the session on time. Somehow I ended up with a group of execs, most of whom were at least twenty years older than me, while across the room Darren and Gabby were in teams with the cool kids.

The execs Rick had introduced me to were in my group, though Rick himself was at a different table.

My group kept glancing my way anytime we were expected to do something. This whole *having a revolutionary idea* makes it difficult to fly under the radar. Also, it's not like Teams for Teamwork required a high IQ to participate. At one point, we literally had to stand up and do our best superhero pose.

How was this a good use of company funds?

During a fifteen-minute break, I took my empty travel cup and was going to refill my coffee in peace, but last night's execs followed me.

"I just love how your brain works," said Male Exec.

"Um..."—*how am I supposed to reply to that?*—"thanks."

"As a kid, did you do well in school?" Female Exec asked.

I couldn't help it. I turned to face her. Had she really just asked how my grades were in elementary school?

"I was a finger-painting prodigy," I said.

Both of the execs laughed—though I hadn't meant it to be funny.

From across the room, Darren raised his eyebrows. It was code for, *Careful, one of the execs might be trying to kill you.*

I raised my shoulder in a half shrug.

Aside from making sure they didn't spike my coffee with rat poison, what was I supposed to do? Check their pockets for feathers?

If one of the execs was trying to kill me, a hotel in Phoenix was their best opportunity to get close to me. I'm not sure which cities they were from, but neither of them worked at our Seattle branch.

I glanced at them. But both were dressed like forgettable corporate drones. I'd like to think I bring a sense of style when dressed for work, but these two looked like they were stock photo models.

Apparently Darren didn't trust me to successfully stay unmurdered by myself because he walked up with his millionaire grin that got him a date whenever he wanted.

"How are we doing?" he asked. "Is Holt staying out of trouble?"

Neither exec looked at all surprised by Darren.

"Holt's keeping *us* out of trouble," said Male Exec.

"We were the first team to have our acronym for VISIBILITY, all thanks to Holt," Female Exec said.

"Is that so?" Darren asked, and he raised an eyebrow when they weren't looking.

There's a chance I'd been complaining about all the stupid acronyms you need to come up with during a layover in Denver and Juniper had utilized the internet to write out some options. Can I help it that Juniper was bored and it was a long layover?

According to my sister, VISIBILITY stands for: *Vision, Inviting, Stunning, Inventive, Brilliant, Impactful, Legendary, Irreproachable, Transformative, Yes!*

I also had acronyms for SYNERGY, REVOLUTIONIZE, and CHANGE up my sleeve. Who knows, they might come in handy for future sessions. Though if anyone expected me to know what the letters in BECKS stood for, I'd be lost.

"I've had the honor of knowing Holt for quite some time." Darren somehow said the words with a straight face—though he'd previously never mentioned *the honor* of my acquaintance. "When did you first hear about him?"

Female Exec froze, her eyes darting up like she was thinking very hard about that magical moment she'd learned of my existence.

"It was sort of roundabout," Male Exec said.

Darren looked super interested as he asked, "How so?"

"Well, I first heard the proposition to close the South Dakota plant. I asked why we'd close it, and I was told it was because Holt Jacobs, one of our engineers, had created a process that bypassed our current technology. I was"—the exec smiled politely—"impressed."

"He is impressive," Darren agreed.

Female Exec was about to give her answer, but I asked, "Are they repurposing the plant?"

"Uh…" Male Exec looked at Female Exec, who shook her head.

She said, "Not that I know of."

I closed my eyes. Suddenly it was super clear why someone might want me dead. I'd known the plant was closing, yet I hadn't bothered to connect the dots. Because of me, hundreds of people would lose their jobs. That was a pretty good reason to want revenge.

My eyes locked with Darren's, but he had yet to reach the same conclusion.

Assuming my hunch was correct, it really wasn't fair. I had nothing to do with the decision to close the plant. Shutting down what might easily be an entire town's livelihood was above my pay grade.

Was there something else the plant could manufacture? For a moment—granted, a very brief moment—I was more concerned about a hundred layoffs than someone trying to kill me. Did that make me a good person?

"Holt?" Rick had joined the group at some point and had clearly just asked me a question, but I had no idea what.

"Excuse me," I said, and handed Darren my coffee. With the conference about to resume, no one questioned me as I beelined for the public restrooms. Once there, I rinsed my face with cool water. I'd become clammy with sweat. After considering the real-world cost of my new idea, thinking about the raise, bonus, and larger office left me feeling queasy.

But really, what was I supposed to do? Part of my job is to make processes more streamlined. If it wasn't me who created a better process, it would be someone else. Maybe my hunch was wrong. I've never been to South Dakota. Could a stranger really want me dead over something I had no control over?

Yet, thinking over past murders I've solved, there was never a good reason for stealing someone's life.

"Holt?" Darren walked into the men's room and handed me the coffee. "Gabby sent me. It's starting."

I nodded. I'd planned on telling Darren about my newest theory, but if I didn't leave now, Gabby would be marching in...or she'd send Rick. Either way, it was best to immediately return to the session.

Gabby's comments about me and Britt came to mind. Was Juniper right about a secret crush? Yet another thing I needed to talk about with Darren, but since Gabby was waiting for us in the hallway, I couldn't exactly ask at the moment.

"He must keep you busy," Darren winked at Gabby—more of an ingrained habit of flirting than any real motive.

"I...uhh..." Gabby gave half a nod and began walking.

What was that about?

I raised an eyebrow at Darren, who shook his head.

When we entered the meeting room, Rick was already on the podium giving introductory remarks, but not everyone was sitting. Darren and I went to our separate tables, and I prepared myself to be bored.

Rick was saying, "...here to tell us more about it are Sasha Redding and Drew MacIntire."

The two execs who'd been fangirling me the whole trip came onto the small stage.

I took a gulp of coffee. This might get interesting.

After the obligatory bad joke that got forced chuckles from about half the attendees, the two execs began talking about investing for retirement.

Not what I'd expected.

I tried to spot a program listing the day's events on the table. Was explaining the difference between a Roth and a traditional IRA really how we were going to spend the afternoon?

My eyes began watering, and I stifled a yawn. If this talk were given in the auditorium, I'd sleep through it for sure. But since I was in a fully lit room, I pretended to be a good employee who paid attention—I even jotted a few notes.

Don't get me wrong. I'm all for setting money aside for retirement. That's why I signed up for the company's 401K plan when I was hired. But I'd already signed up. Did I really need to hear all the information repeated?

About halfway through the session, instead of just telling us about compounding interest, they called up some of the attendees to perform a little skit to show the value of investing early on.

I'm pretty good at becoming invisible when volunteers are needed—there's a slight chance I *accidentally* dropped a pen and ducked under the table at the right time.

Once the two execs had finished calling people up, there were thirteen *volunteers* onstage. Darren, Gabby, and Rick were among the unlucky ones...though it didn't seem like any of them minded.

This is where it got weird. All thirteen of them were given different-sized bottles of bubbles. Like the kind of bubbles my nephew would spill all over my pants.

Gabby was at the bottom of the line, holding a mini bottle with a tiny wand—the type given out at weddings. She was instructed to try to blow as many bubbles as far as possible in ten seconds.

While Gabby did her best, her resources were limited.

"See Gabby's waited until sixty-four to start investing," the Male Exec said. "At this point her money can't go as far, and most of it will be put in less risky but also less lucrative bonds."

Darren was next to Gabby with a slightly bigger bottle. When instructed, he was able to create a few more bubbles that went slightly farther.

"Darren's started investing at sixty," the Female Exec said. "His money is getting a better chance to grow, but he still has limited resources."

I shifted in my chair. If anything, this session was making me re-think whether I should be investing. The way they'd dumbed it down made it feel like they were recommending I be the bottom tier of a pyramid scheme. And were they really going to go through this cheesy process with eleven more people?

They did.

But what was the point? I'm almost thirty-one. It's not like I can go back in time and start investing at an earlier age.

Rick stood near the end of the line with a fairly large bottle of bubbles. My guess is he represented someone my age.

Female Exec was just wrapping up the person before Rick with how far you could go investing five percent of your income in your midthirties when Rick's phone buzzed.

"Sorry," he said. "I'll silence it." But once he read the screen, his face turned almost gray. "Excuse me." Rick left the platform still holding his container of bubbles. "Holt"—he set the bottle in front of me—"get up there." Then his face hardened, and he answered his phone with, "This is Rick Olson," and he left.

I looked down at the bottle. I'd been so careful not to be voluntold to get up onstage, and now this happened.

I would have ignored Rick's request and hidden the bottle under the table, but somehow everyone's eyes were on me.

"Come on up, Holt," Male Exec said.

I nodded and stood slowly from my seat. This didn't need to be a big deal. I'd go up there and join the parade of people blowing bubbles.

"Now, Holt, would you mind telling us how old you are?" Female Exec asked.

For the record, I did mind. My age isn't particularly private information. Still, it wasn't anyone's business to know. But if I didn't answer, people would make it into a big deal, so I said, "Thirty."

"Perfect," the Female Exec said. "Now, Holt's thirty, and he's also representing someone who starts investing at thirty."

"Go ahead and make as many bubbles as you can when you're ready," Male Exec said, holding his phone with the stopwatch app open.

I tried to unscrew the bottle, but it had one of those childproof twisty locks on. It took some finagling before I got the cap to move. Heat crept up my face as the seconds ticked by. In reality it didn't take very long. Still, you don't want your coworkers thinking you can't figure out a childproof lid.

The moment the seal gave way, I tore off the lid. In my speed, some of the liquid sloshed over my hands.

The color of it made me drop the bottle.

Instead of clear soapy liquid, the contents were deep red, like blood.

There was a stunned silence as the dark red liquid spilled across the stage. I half expected one of the execs to say, *Ah yes. That represents a market crash!*

They didn't.

CHAPTER 9

I sniffed my hands. Instead of smelling metallic, it had a sweet scent, more like fruit punch. There was also something wrong with the color and consistency. It had to be fake blood.

"Did one of you plan this?" Darren asked the execs, his voice clipped with barely controlled rage.

"No, that..." Male Exec couldn't stop staring at the fake blood puddling on the floor near my feet. "Uh...That wasn't part of the program."

"I'll call the police," Darren said.

"Already dialing," said Gabby with the phone at her ear.

This may have been overstepping, but I was standing on a platform in a room full of people staring at me while my shared assistant called the police. "All right." I raised my hands—trying to ignore the red streaks. "We'll be ending this session early. Point is, invest for retirement now and reap compounding interest later."

No one moved.

Darren took a step toward me. "I'm sure Sasha and Drew would be more than happy to answer any questions later on in the conference. Plus, if you want to update your 401K, you can do that by clicking on the *retirement* option on your employee web portal."

Somewhere in the back somebody sneezed, but otherwise no one moved.

It took Male Exec saying, "Go enjoy the sunshine," for the attendees to begin slowly shuffling out.

As everyone left, I crouched down to examine the bottle floating slightly in the red liquid. Since it was representing someone who started investing relatively young, the opening was fairly big.

On a hunch, I moved around the puddle to see inside.

While most of the fake blood had spilled out, the container wasn't empty. There was a strange silver object inside. Gingerly, I took a pen from my suit coat, doing my best not to get fake blood on my clothes. Using my pen, I moved the bottle out of the puddle.

I crouched on my knees and bent until I was eye level with the bottle and could take a better look. I slid the pen inside and moved the silver item until I was satisfied I knew what it was.

"What is it?" Darren asked.

Since I had an audience, I shrugged and said, "No idea."

Darren looked at me a moment longer, than gave a slight nod, having figured out *no idea* was code for *I'll tell you later*.

"Ah, Mr. Jacobs. Good to see you again," Detective Bunny said as she entered the Sun Room.

"That was quick," I said.

The detective waved her hand. "I was already here on other business."

Other business? What kind of other business? Were they looking more into yesterday's death by stage light? Or was she investigating today's pillow butchering or the vague email threat?

If Juniper were here, she'd find a way to get Detective Bunny to tell her, but since I'm not that charismatic, I didn't bother trying to interrogate the police detective.

Detective Bunny walked right past Darren, and neither one of them acknowledged the other.

"Is there something else inside that bottle?" she asked since I was still crouched half-bent toward it.

"Yeah."

"I see." She put on a pair of gloves and got an evidence bag the size of a grocery sack. She took the bubble bottle from my hands and frowned at the added weight. "It's heavy."

"Uh-huh." I should have noticed the added weight when I was trying to open the lid. "It's a message," I added.

Male Exec let out a cry from where he sat with his head in his hands. When everyone looked his way, he said, "Invest in your future. That's all this afternoon was supposed to be. Now there's police and blood everywhere."

"Fake blood," I couldn't help adding—though actually, I didn't know for certain that the blood wasn't real.

"Are we sure it's fake?" Gabby asked, her face paler than usual.

"We'll get it tested," Detective Bunny said. "But I'm confident it's fake. Real blood is thicker."

Everyone else in the room relaxed at that. Funny, I'd said the blood was fake, but no one believed it until a police detective said so.

What followed was Detective Bunny finding out who all had touched the bottle. I'd been the last person to after Rick. Gabby had helped hand out the bottles. Female Exec had stored all the bubbles in her hotel room, while Male Exec had been the one to order them online and bring them to the hotel.

It was all a little much. I was about to run a hand through my hair when the red of the fake blood caught my attention.

"Can I go wash up?" I asked.

The detective nodded, and I excused myself to the restroom.

While I scrubbed my hands for a good minute, not all of the red washed away. Not only did someone want me dead, but now I also had dyed hands. It shouldn't matter, but must my hands be stained red?

I wasn't in a rush to rejoin the police interview—or see the puddle of fake blood. Instead, I texted Britt: *Hope this will finish early. Can we meet at your spa for dinner?*

After sending the text, I realized that might have sounded romantic when in reality I had a work BFF named Darren who'd probably tag along.

Which was actually strange. On previous trips Darren spent most of his free time flirting, and we only sat together during sessions. Was he sticking around more because he was worried about my safety?

I decided to send Britt a clarifying text: *I'm probably bringing someone.*

Britt hadn't replied to my original text, but her answer to my second text was almost instantaneous.

Britt: *You bringing Gabby?*

I rolled my eyes, pretty sure she was joking, but either way it felt too soon. I replied with a GIF of an animated gerbil saying, *Very funny.* Then I sent one word: *Darren.*

Brittany didn't bother with words but sent the always classy thumbs-up emoji.

After putting away my phone, I saw my reflection in the bathroom mirror. My face had an out-of-control grin. Was it because of Britt? If I stayed with her too long, I might get smile wrinkles.

I was so happy, I'd sort of forgotten about the *Mystery of the Bloody Bubbles.* When I left the restroom, it all came back to me. Detective Bunny was standing on the other side of the hallway carrying a large evidence bag.

She gave a professional nod. "I thought you'd run off."

I shrugged. "Nope. I got distracted texting my girlfriend."

Detective Bunny nodded. "Is she worried?"

What? Why would Brittany be worried?

Sensing my confusion, she added, "Because of—" and she held up the evidence bag.

Oh.

Right.

"Yeah"—I shifted on my feet—"I kind of didn't tell her."

"I see," Detective Bunny said, but it was her turn to look confused.

I ran a hand through my hair. No need to get defensive or say something stupid trying to prove I wasn't a bad boyfriend. "We were making dinner plans."

Detective Bunny blinked before unlocking her tablet. That was the cue that we'd shifted from casual small talk and were now back to business.

"You said the metal in the bottle was a message. What makes you think that?"

Tension began to burn between my temples. Given how many police interviews I've been a part of, you'd think I'd be more used to it. I tilted my head in the direction of a small seating area off the hallway and asked, "Can we sit down?"

"Of course," she said.

We sat opposite each other. I took a deep breath. I might sound like I was bragging when I explained the situation. "For starters," I said, not able to meet her eyes, "I'm kind of the reason my company is now saving a lot of money."

I stopped talking, too worried about how arrogant I'd sounded.

Detective Bunny looked up from her tablet. "Go on," she said, apparently unbothered by my humblebrag.

"I was able to simplify a process, eliminating the need for one part. There was a plant in South Dakota where all it did was manufacture…" I pointed to the evidence bag.

She raised the bag. "This part?"

"Yup."

"And this part you made obsolete ended up at the bottom of a bottle of fake blood that you were told to open?"

I sat back in my chair. "Not to be overly paranoid, but it felt targeted."

"I can see how you'd reach that conclusion." Detective Bunny tapped the tablet with her finger. "And what's happening to the manufacturing plant now?"

"As far as I know there's nothing official, but everyone thinks it's getting shut down."

"*Holt must pay,*" Detective Bunny said so quietly I almost missed it.

"Something like that," I said.

"Any guesses on who would do this?"

I shook my head. "Rick was the one who handed me the bottle. But even if he does want me dead, filling a bottle with fake blood is way too theatrical for him. He's more of a knife to the heart kind of guy." The moment the words were out, I regretted them. What kind of psycho tells a police officer that a potential suspect is more of a *knife to the heart kind of guy*?

"Well, all right." Detective Bunny stood, and I couldn't tell if she was amused or offended. "I'll talk to the chief and see if we can get you some sort of protective detail."

Protective detail? Juniper would make so much fun of me if that happened. Plus, if anyone on my detail happened to be an attractive woman, it'd probably turn into drama. Overall, not worth it.

"Not necessary," I said.

The area around Detective Bunny's eyes tightened. "It's your life," she said.

I tried not to read too much into her word choice and thanked her as she left. With that, it seemed one more mishap had been handled. I went back to the Sun Room and found Darren sitting alone at a table by the exit. "I figured you'd come back here," he said.

"Do you want to meet up with the girls for supper?" I asked. "I need to get out of here."

"Give me five minutes to change," Darren said, already removing his cuff links.

We met back in the lobby closer to ten minutes later. We were both wearing board shorts and polos—though the colors in my outfit were more monochromatic than Darren's.

When Darren saw me, he let out a low whistle. "Okay. You have to go back and change. We don't need to be matching."

I ignored him and instead walked toward the exit. "Let's just hurry before Rick can stop us."

Once Darren and I had an Uber, I called Brittany and told her we were on our way.

Britt said they'd meet us out front, and the line went dead right as my sister started complaining about not having enough time to get ready. But when the vehicle pulled up, Juniper was standing next to Britt looking as effortlessly perfect as she always did.

Juniper walked to the driver's window and waited for him to unroll it. "Would you recommend Montaveyos?"

At first the man didn't answer, too stunned by getting the full force of Juniper's attention. Finally he was able to squeak out, "Yes."

"Wonderful. I'll put Montaveyos as our destination in the app." Juniper rewarded him with a smile before climbing into the back seat.

After the car started moving, I texted Juniper: *What was that for?*

She texted back: *What was what for?*

I rolled my eyes. Juniper knew her effect on men—especially when she gave them her full attention.

Speaking of male attention, Juniper was missing her main companion.

Me: *Where's Chouzie?*

Juniper: *At the spa. He needed quiet time to decompress.*

I sent a GIF of a bratty kid saying, *I'm sooo jealous.*

Knowing Juniper, I was worried she'd choose some overly trendy spot that was packed with whatever the current version of hipsters is called. While Montaveyos definitely catered to a younger clientele, it had dim lighting and was more the sexy spot you'd take a date you wanted to impress. We were seated at a dark booth in the back corner...probably because Darren and I were underdressed in our board shorts.

Once our drinks were ordered, I stretched my arm around Britt and let out a sigh.

"What's wrong with your hand?" she asked, examining my fingers, which were resting by her shoulder.

My hand. Of course Britt spotted the red dye. I'd planned on telling both of them about my newest mishap. But it had been so nice to pretend nothing was wrong that I'd wanted the act to continue a little longer.

I tried to avoid the question. "Uh, the bruises on my forearm are from when Darren squeezed me too hard after the stage light fell."

"Holt." Britt waited until I looked at her. "I asked about your hand."

"Well"—I removed my arm so I could face her better—"there was another incident."

Darren snorted. "That's an understatement."

"Fine," I said. "Then you tell the story."

If I was guilty of underselling dropping a bottle full of fake blood, Darren was guilty of overselling. At one point during the retelling, Brittany gripped my arm because she was so caught up in the moment.

"...but blood wasn't the only thing this rancid bottle held." Darren flourished his hands like a magician. "No, something else lay at the bottom. Something too awful to be named."

"What was it?" Juniper asked, her whole body quivering with excitement.

Darren shrugged, suddenly dropping the act. "I don't know. Holt wouldn't tell me."

Suddenly I had three sets of eyes on me. Before I could frame words into sentences, our waitress returned with our drinks.

"Ready to order?"

"No," Juniper and Britt said in unison.

But I said, "Yes."

"Holt"—my sister pouted her bottom lip—"please."

"I barely ate lunch and I'm starving." I proceeded to order.

Juniper could wait to hear what the mysterious item was until after we'd all ordered. And it wasn't even that mysterious. In fact, I'd spent the better part of a year knowing all the components of that one tiny part.

I don't think Juniper read the menu, just ordered the first entrée she saw—which would explain why she ordered a dish featuring boiled cabbage. Surprisingly unsexy, given the trendy restaurant.

"So?" Juniper asked, while our waitress was writing down Britt's order.

"It was—" I started to say.

"Tell it like Darren," Juniper begged.

I rolled my eyes but did change my voice and used my hands to be more theatrical. "Lying at the bottom of the bottle was the piece of manufacturing equipment our handsome hero had rendered obsolete."

Juniper snorted. "Please."

Brittany was a good enough girlfriend not to laugh at the *handsome hero* comment, but her lips trembled like she really wanted to.

Darren completely ignored the comment, instead zeroing in on the facts. "Leaving that piece behind would imply your assassin hates you because of your recent discoveries."

"Correct," I said.

"Hold on," Juniper said, a fruity cocktail halfway to her lips. "You're both forgetting about one important detail." My sister stopped talking, but when neither Darren nor I begged her to explain, she went on without any encouragement. "There was blood. Blood goes through your heart. Brokenhearted. Holt's lovesick stalker assistant."

"She's not a stalker," Darren and I both said.

"Of course she's not," Juniper said, but she winked at Britt when she thought we weren't looking.

"How easy would it be to get one of those parts?" Brittany asked.

"What! This isn't about the machinery. The blood's the important part." Juniper would have stood, but she was trapped in a booth with Darren blocking her exit. "The blood shows it's about love. That other thing was just a ruse."

"A ruse?" I sat back. "No way."

Juniper tapped a manicured finger to her mouth. "I have an idea on how to prove I'm right."

I groaned.

Juniper having an idea meant one thing. Trouble.

CHAPTER 10

"What if you're wrong about Gabby?" Darren asked.

Juniper ignored the question. "Imagine some-one—no, that's too vague—imagine Gabby is madly in love with Holt."

I groaned.

"Why can't poor Gabby capture the man of her dreams?" Juniper continued.

"He has a girlfriend," Britt said, squeezing my hand.

"Correct," Juniper said, tapping her nose. "What if—"

"*And*," I interrupted, "I'm her boss. Even if I were available, it would be inappropriate for us to be in a relationship."

Juniper actually laughed. "Please, Holt, you need to relax. Bosses date their assistants all the time."

I shook my head. "No, they don't."

"Sure, they do." Darren's eyes sparkled. "Assistants date their bosses all the time on reality TV."

Juniper decided to ignore us, turning her whole attention to Brittany. "Like I said, the *only* reason Gabby couldn't date Holt is he's in a relationship." She clapped her hands together, overexcited with her brilliance. "But what if Holt suddenly became single?"

I shifted so there wasn't any space between Britt and me. "The only way I become single is if Britt and I break up, which isn't happening."

My words had an unexpected growl to them. A faint blush worked its way up Brittany's cheeks as she snuggled even closer.

"Please, Holt," my sister said patronizingly. "All I'm suggesting is staging a breakup to give Gabby the impression that you're available."

"No," I said. "Absolutely not. Brittany and I aren't going to break up just because you're bored on vacation."

"*Fake* break up," Juniper said like that made all the difference. "You're not willing to pretend to split with Brittany if it could save your life?"

Darren shook his head. "I don't see how that's going to save Holt's life."

"And I'm not dying," I added, a little too loudly given the romantic atmosphere.

Britt didn't move away from me, but she asked, "How would a fake breakup help Holt?"

I bowed my head. The writing was on the wall. Pretty soon my persuasive sister would convince Britt, and once she agreed...well, Brittany could get me to do anything.

I must've interrupted Juniper when I asked, "If Gabby's so in love with me she wants to kill me—" I hesitated. Saying that out loud really highlighted how stupid that idea was.

"If she can't have Holt nobody can," Darren muttered.

"Right," I said. "Even if that's all true, how would me being single prove any of that?"

"Yeah," Darren agreed. "It's not like Gabby would confess her undying love the same day Holt dumped his girlfriend. Holt would need time to recover."

"Oh, I don't know"—Juniper tossed her hair and batted her eyes—"he'd need a shoulder to cry on."

"Nope!" I would have left our booth, but I was still wrapped around Britt.

"How would we do it?" Brittany asked, sitting up.

Juniper scrunched up her nose as she paused to think. "Well, it would need to be public—something with a lot of witnesses so everyone would gossip about it."

Had my sister just suggested I stage a fight so everyone I knew could discuss my personal business? My stomach knotted at the thought of such a nightmare.

"Also, you'd need to plan the main points of your breakup ahead of time," Juniper added.

Brittany nodded like that was an obvious step for staged breakups.

I raised an eyebrow at Darren. Was any of this making sense to him?

He shrugged and asked, "Why's that?"

"Because if you're not careful, a fake fight can quickly turn into the real thing," Juniper said.

I rubbed a hand along my jaw. "And which teen movie are you basing this off?"

"All of them," Darren said.

We both chuckled, but Britt and Juniper remained serious.

"It does help that Holt yelled, *Are you dumping me* last night," Juniper said.

"I was just thinking that," Britt agreed. "It will make it more believable."

"As for the talking points..." Juniper trailed off as she stared at me. "Any ideas?"

Was I really supposed to come up with a pretend reason to dump Britt? "I could say the sight of her makes me want to vomit."

Juniper's eyes widened. "In this case, maybe less is more."

"Good point," Britt said.

Before I could get too insulted with them dismissing my idea, the food arrived. The portions were small and the prices high, but at least everything tasted good.

"Let me see your schedule," Juniper said halfway through the meal.

I texted Juniper the revised schedule Gabby had sent over. Darren, Brittany, and I resumed an earlier conversation from the flight about which beverage is best at hot, cold, and lukewarm temperatures while Juniper squinted down at her phone like she was about to crack a top-secret cipher.

"Got it!" she announced. "Brittany and I will have to move our sugar scrub to eleven, but that's easily done. At ten, Holt is scheduled to be in the lobby to leave for some golf thing. Holt and Brittany will ride down the elevator at nine forty-seven, and when the doors open, the two of them will apparently be mid-fight. Brittany will yell, *It's over*, and storm off. Then—bam—Holt's a free agent."

"And this will prove what exactly?" Darren asked.

Juniper didn't answer the question. "Now Holt makes sure to act upset after it happens."

I raised an eyebrow. "I'm going on a field trip to a golf course while everyone at work gossips about me getting dumped? Trust me, it won't be an act."

"Great," Juniper said, totally ignoring the sarcasm.

Once supper was over we walked around the nearby streets, just hanging out. Maybe this was overly clingy, but it felt like I hadn't seen Britt in days. It was past my bedtime when we called it a night. We dropped the girls off at the spa before returning to the Camelback Hotel.

In the elevator, Darren pushed the button for the seventh floor. Since he hadn't bothered with my floor, I pressed the button for the twentieth floor.

"What do you think you're doing?" Darren asked.

Wasn't it obvious? I was so tired, my eyes were watering. Still, I was polite enough to answer. "I'm going to bed."

"You're not sleeping in that room." Darren said it as a statement.

The image of my bedroom full of massacred feathers stopped me mid-yawn. "It'll be fine. Probably," I said—while secretly wondering if I could call Detective Bunny and accept her offer of a bodyguard. "I always put the extra lock on the door when I'm inside."

The elevator doors opened for Darren's floor, but he didn't get out.

"What are you doing?" I asked.

"I'll help you pack all your junk and bring it down to my room."

"You want a roommate?"

Darren shook his head and may have muttered something about me needing more coffee. "Don't make a big deal about this," he said. "We were always planning on sharing a room. I have an extra bed. And I'm a much lighter sleeper. If there's trouble, I'd wake up."

"Darren"—I grinned—"I had no idea you'd like to keep me alive. Come on. Let's hug it out."

I stretched my arms open. Unfortunately, I'd pushed Darren too far. Instead of walking away, he caught me in a bear hug that almost knocked the wind out of me. "Stop it," I said, struggling to speak with barely any air.

When Darren let go, he marched me to my suite. I ended up brushing my teeth in my bathroom before packing everything and going down to Darren's. I knew it was way less fancy than my suite. Still, I let out a groan when I walked into the small room with the two queen-size beds.

Darren held up a hand. "If you can't say anything nice about me saving your butt, just go to bed."

Since there was nothing nice to say, I lay down without any other comments. The covers were up around my neck and my eyes were half-closed when I noticed Darren sitting at the room's tiny desk with his laptop open.

Strange. He's usually up late socializing.

"Don't stay in the room because of me," I said. "No one will try to kill me in the next few hours."

"What?" Darren asked, swiveling around in the chair—there's a chance I'd been mumbling.

"Go make friends," I said. "I promise not to be murdered until you come back."

Darren's face was half-amused, but there was another emotion I couldn't place. "Nah," he said. "I don't feel like going out tonight."

I nodded, trying to figure out why Darren was acting so strangely. I knew I should have the answer. I just needed to put together all the pieces. Who knows what I would have figured out. But my eyelids were too heavy to keep open. Once they slid shut, I fell asleep.

Pounding on the door woke me out of a dead sleep. Was that my killer?

The room was completely dark. In the other bed, Darren gave a snort as he woke up. "What's happening?" he asked as the knocking continued.

"You're my bodyguard. Shouldn't you know?" I asked. I stumbled out of bed and crept to the peephole.

"It's Rick," I whisper-shouted at Darren, hoping my boss wouldn't hear.

"What does he want?" Darren asked, sounding groggy.

"What do you want?" I called through the door.

Immediately the knocking stopped. "Holt, you're late for the CEO's breakfast."

Breakfast?

"What time is it?" I asked Darren.

In the darkness I could hear Darren fumbling for his phone. "It's six oh seven."

No, no, no, no, no.

As it turns out—assuming Rick wasn't planning to kill me—the only person better than my murderer at tracking my movements was my boss.

He'd shown up at my hideaway because I was seven minutes late for the all-important breakfast.

"Are you dressed?" Rick asked through the door.

"Give me a minute," I called and began rushing around the room as Rick grumbled complaints in the hallway.

I clicked on the closest lamp in my mad scramble for a suit.

"Turn the light off when you leave," Darren mumbled, covering his face with a pillow.

Once dressed, I quickly added gel to my hair and smoothed it back. I decided to skip shaving. One, I pulled off sexy stubble. Two, Rick had resumed knocking on the door. I slid on my shoes and didn't bother with the laces. Those could be fixed in the elevator. After grabbing my phone and conference lanyard, I left the room.

Unfortunately, I didn't have time to turn off the light. Though if Darren's low snoring was any indication, the light wasn't keeping him from falling back asleep.

Some bodyguard.

Rick stepped away from the door when it swung open. "Took you long enough," he said.

For the record, I'd done all of that in under three minutes, but I kept my mouth shut. I matched Rick's half jog to the elevators while trying not to trip on my loose shoelaces.

One shoe was tied before the elevator arrived, and once inside I knelt to get the other shoe.

"How did you find me?"

"Gabby told me," Rick said.

My spine tingled as alarms went off. Gabby knew where I was? Could she just be very good at her job, or was she stalking me? Then again, it wouldn't be much of a leap to guess I'd be hiding out in Darren's room.

"Holt."

"Yeah?"

"Did you hear me?"

I shook my head.

"What I was saying," Rick overenunciated, "was I want you on your best behavior."

I couldn't stop the eye roll.

But Rick kept talking. "That means smiling and answering questions."

"I haven't had any coffee."

"Drink some at breakfast. This is important."

With my second shoe tied, I had my hand on the elevator rail and was about to stand up when a yawn caught me off guard. With it came a horrifying discovery. In my rush to get ready this morning, I'd forgotten to brush my teeth.

I was about to have breakfast with the CEO and a bunch of VPs with morning breath.

My hand was still on the elevator rail and I was going to pull myself up when a tremble shook the tiny room.

"Rick?" I asked.

He didn't answer, but from his suddenly gray face and the way he'd begun gripping the rail, he'd also felt it.

Just then, the elevator gave a violent tremble before jolting to a stop. The main light shut off, and emergency lights began to glow, casting eerie shadows in the small space. Rick let out a groan before sinking to the floor beside me.

We were going to miss the CEO's breakfast.

CHAPTER 11

For all the time I've spent riding up and down elevators, I've never actually been stuck in one.

I glanced at Rick, hoping he'd take charge and press the elevator call button. My boss's eyes had grown cloudy, and he was panting. Not only was I going to have to make the call, but I was trapped in a room with someone having a panic attack.

Fantastic.

First, I pressed the emergency button. Second, I crouched in front of Rick and loosened his tie before undoing the top two buttons on his shirt.

"Camelback Hotel, are you trapped in an elevator?" a woman's disembodied voice asked.

"Uh, yeah, my name is Holt Jacobs. I'm stuck in your elevator."

"Which elevator?"

Really? This was an in-house call system. Shouldn't it say which elevator I was in?

"Uhh..." I could dimly make out a sticker with the number *one* over the doors. "We're in elevator one."

"Is anyone injured?" the voice asked.

"Not really," I said, since Rick looking wildly around the room with his tongue partially hanging out wasn't really an injury.

"All right, Holt, we'll send someone right over."

I started to say, "Thanks," but the line clicked off. "Great," I muttered.

Rick began clawing weakly at my arms. "There's no air," he whispered between fast shallow breaths.

I squeezed my eyes shut. This was a situation that Brittany would have handled like a champ. Meanwhile, I was irritated. Not so much at Rick for having a panic attack, but more the fact that I was the only one present to deal with it—plus, I still hadn't had any coffee.

"All right," I said, making my voice sound confident so he'd think I knew what I was doing. "Come on. Take some deep breaths. In." I inhaled deeply. "And out." I exhaled.

Rick didn't immediately calm down, but gradually his breathing slowed and some of the terror left his eyes—which was handy since all the deep breathing was leaving me lightheaded.

I sat back against the wall beside Rick. Sweat was forming along my temples, and at least one bead of sweat had rolled down my spine. Also, the air had a heaviness to it. That's when I figured out we weren't getting any airflow. We weren't about to suffocate, but who knew how long we'd be trapped in a poor man's sauna.

"You might want to take off your suit jacket," I said as I removed my jacket and tie.

Rick fumbled at the jacket's one button before giving up. While he'd calmed down considerably from when we'd first gotten stuck, his hands were trembling too hard to undo the button.

"Here," I said. I undid the button and helped ease the jacket off his shoulders.

"Sorry," he said.

I shrugged. "Could happen to anyone."

"No, Holt. I'm sorry about how I've treated you this whole trip."

I raised my eyebrows. It was like I was about to hear a deathbed confession, but as it stood, we weren't even in danger.

"There were rumors I might be *encouraged* to take an early retirement. Or"—Rick shuddered—"some remote consulting gig."

I nodded. The *remote consulting* he was referring to wasn't the dream job of someone who just wanted to set their own hours and travel. This was being sent out to pasture when Human Resources said there wasn't just cause for firing. For Rick, who'd spent decades working at BECKS, it would be a major slap in the face.

"Your discovery couldn't have come at a better time," Rick continued. "They'd actually scheduled a meeting with me and the board when you marched into my office." He shook his head. "It was like you'd handed me a golden ticket. I'm sorry it took almost dying in an elevator for me to tell you."

Almost dying was definitely an exaggeration, but I didn't need to point that out.

"That's why you've been so...involved this trip?"

Rick nodded and actually seemed ashamed. "I've done everything I could think of to remind everyone here I'm an asset to this company. And"—his eye twitched—"the famous Holt Jacobs is my employee." That made sense. Rick had been very underfoot.

The elevator shifted slightly, and I managed not to react.

"Did you feel that?" Rick's eyes were panicked.

"No," I lied. "Relax. We're perfectly safe."

Perfectly safe wasn't completely accurate, but there was no need to give Rick a second panic attack. Plus, I was trying to shut off the engineer portion of my brain. Because really, I didn't have enough information. I didn't want a cable to snap and drop thirty floors. But if that happened, I'd be dead by the bottom.

Besides, that option seemed unlikely. Really, the best choice was to stay calm and wait it out.

With nothing else to do, I began processing everything I'd just learned.

Rick had been using my discovery to keep his job, which made him an unlikely suspect for wanting me dead.

I glanced up at the video camera in the upper-right corner of the ceiling. Had this elevator breaking down been unfortunate luck, or was this the work of my assassin? Again, the problem with a workplace conference full of engineers is that it would be relatively easy for any of them to watch the live video feed and once I was in the elevator shut it down.

Really, it might be better if it were a case of simple tampering instead of mechanical failure. If all that happened was the elevator getting shut off, hopefully it wouldn't take a genius to turn it back on.

I rested my head against the wall and closed my eyes. This whole being stalked and toyed with was getting old. Granted, I didn't actually know if the elevator breaking was the work of my killer, but what were the chances they were unrelated?

Rick's phone began ringing. How did he have service in the elevator? Maybe it was because we were stuck in one spot.

"This is Rick." He sounded way more authoritative than he looked, all ashen and sweaty. "Yes, I'm with Holt. We're trapped in—"

Rick must've been interrupted. He stayed silent listening to the other end. He sounded deflated when he replied. "We'll do our best to drop in on the breakfast, but it all depends on whether they fix the elevator."

It seemed the caller hung up abruptly without saying goodbye.

Rick sighed as he slid the phone back into his pocket. "You've been missed."

I nodded.

A new thought began taking shape. If being trapped meant I didn't have to attend the breakfast, maybe it wasn't so bad.

Then again, was my killer keeping me from going to the CEO's breakfast? What did they think would happen if I went?

After a few more minutes, I tried to call Brittany. All I got was her voicemail. She probably wasn't up yet, though depending on their schedule, she and Juniper might be mid–mud bath.

After I left a voicemail, there wasn't much to do. I was sweating in a small room with my boss, while growing increasingly desperate for coffee. I glanced at the elevator's *call* button. Would there be a way for them to deliver coffee while I was trapped inside?

Catching my eye movement, Rick actually leaned over and pressed the button.

"Any updates?" he asked after the expected introductions.

"Well..." This disembodied voice was a male bass. "There have been some complications."

At *complications*, Rick grabbed my arm—right where Darren had bruised it yesterday.

"Can't you just open the elevator doors?" Rick's voice was high and a little squeaky.

There was silence on the line for a few seconds before the answer came. "No. You're stuck between floors."

I asked, "Do you have an estimate of when we'll get out?"

"Not exactly," the voice said. "Sit tight."

Rick and I both groaned.

In my rush to get dressed this morning, I'd neglected to put on an undershirt, but if I was going to be trapped in an accidental microwave for an indefinite amount of time, I had to take off my button-up. The shirt was already damp from sweat, and I rested it half-folded over one of the bars. Next I stretched out my legs and began tapping my fingers on the floor. I left my conference lanyard on. For some reason, even stuck in an elevator it felt wrong to take it off.

Was someone trying to teach me a lesson, or was I the mouse and the killer was a cat playing with me before I was killed?

Either option, they'd have to try harder. Really, the biggest inconvenience was not getting any coffee, and there were plenty of ways to withhold coffee that didn't involve shutting down an elevator.

I was about to rest my head in my hands when I got distracted by the streaks of red dye still on them. What was with that bottle of blood?

Who knew the execs would be doing those theatrics with the bubbles? Was this a program they did often? That would make it easier to plan the swapping of soapy water with fake blood.

And how would someone orchestrate me opening the right bottle? If Gabby or Rick had planned the trick, they couldn't control who received the bottle of red blood. If it was either of the execs, they couldn't have planned for Rick to take a phone call. Even if they'd somehow planned that, they wouldn't have known Rick would hand his bottle off to me.

"Who called you?" I asked.

"Huh?"

Apparently I needed to clarify my question. "Yesterday, during the retirement workshop, who called you?"

"Uhh..." Rick's eyes were cloudy. "My wife?"

I waited, hoping he would further explain.

Finally, Rick added, "She was calling from a hospital phone. I normally wouldn't answer during a work event, but the hospital showed up on my caller ID." He rubbed at his arm. "My grandkid broke his arm on the swing."

"Sorry," I mumbled.

Assuming Rick was telling the truth about his grandkid, a broken arm wasn't something anyone at the conference could have planned. There was no way to plan me opening the bloody bottle.

What if I hadn't opened that bottle?

The bottle represented someone my age and had that engineering piece inside. I would have gotten the message without any red dye sloshing over my hands. Also, given my sudden popularity, it would be reasonable for my wannabe-murderer to assume the organizers would try to have me open the bottle that represented my age.

I rested against the wall. One mini-mystery solved. Now, to figure out the rest before I was murdered.

CHAPTER 12

I probably would have fallen asleep while I waited if I'd been by myself. Problem was, with Rick, anytime I was starting to drift off, he'd moan or ask how much longer. Somehow a man I more or less respected had turned into a whiny kid on a car trip.

Time passed by slowly. At around 7:30 a.m. the caffeine headache began forming. At 8:40 a.m. Rick called again and was informed the elevator would be fixed *soon*. At 9:23 a.m. Darren texted: *You good?* with a GIF of a magician trapped in a glass box. Sometime after 9:40 a.m. I'd successfully begun to doze when the ground began moving beneath me.

My head snapped up. This time I asked, "Do you feel that?"

Rick was too busy white-knuckling the rail to answer.

The main lights had turned on, and the floor numbers were blinking for lower and lower floors. This was definitely a controlled decline. It had taken around four hours, but it was finally fixed. I needed to use the restroom and shower, but before anything else, I needed at least two doses of coffee.

When the elevator doors finally opened on the lobby, Rick (rather melodramatically) crawled onto solid ground. For my part, I walked out on my own two feet and only noticed after the doors swung shut that I'd left my clothes in the elevator. I was standing in the lobby, shirtless, with my conference badge hanging around my neck. Worse, with all the sweat, it looked like I'd rubbed myself with baby oil and was parading around in dress pants like I was late for a bachelorette party.

"Um, Mr. Jacobs?" Detective Bunny was waiting for us. Her cheeks were flushed, and she couldn't quite look away from my chest.

At least I pulled off shirtless and sweaty.

"Sorry," I said, pressing the elevator button. The goal was to quickly retrieve my shirt, but the elevator was already eight floors up.

"What happened?" Rick asked.

He didn't pull off being sweaty. If anything, Rick resembled an actor in a commercial experiencing a pre-cardiac episode.

Detective Bunny tore her eyes away from me to tell Rick, "It would be best if I showed you."

We followed her past the check-in desk and into the staff side of the Camelback Hotel. She led us through a maze of hallways and doors until we arrived at the elevator room. A surprising number of people were crammed inside.

Besides the police officers and firefighters, there was a guy who wasn't in as good shape and was dressed like someone whose second home was in virtual reality. My guess, he was the elevator repairman.

Standing beside the elevator room, I noticed the door hadn't been opened but was smashed off its hinges. Maybe I owed the firefighters a thank-you.

Catching my gaze, Detective Bunny nodded. "Yes, the perpetrator managed to wedge the door shut behind them."

That meant two things. First, the elevator getting stuck was intentional. Second, the person was probably attending ENGINEERS OF THE FUTURE IN THE PRESENT, since they'd jammed the door so successfully that firefighters had to break it down.

"But why did it take forever to fix it?" Rick's voice was extra whiny.

"We needed someone who specialized in elevators." Detective Bunny tilted her head toward the man who wasn't a first responder. "Trevor was already on a job when we called, but he was able to come right after."

Somehow I wasn't surprised I'd been left in an elevator while the repairman finished up another call.

"Was it difficult to repair?" I asked the guy.

He shook his head.

I peered into the room. "Do the camera feeds from the elevator play here?"

"Yes," Detective Bunny replied. "It seems likely this is related to your previous incidents."

I nodded. "It's what I figured. Are there clues about who tampered with the elevator?"

"We're looking into it," Detective Bunny said. "But there's fewer security cameras in the staff areas." She shrugged. "I'm not sure what we'll turn up."

In the meantime, I remained a sitting duck.

Great.

My flight out of Phoenix was at 2:00 p.m. tomorrow. I needed to keep myself alive for another twenty-eight hours in Arizona.

Could I completely switch the hotel I was staying in?

Have a spa day with Britt and Juniper. After all, staying alive is more important than having a job.

Then again, if I was at the spa, strangers would be touching me. I barely like it when my family touches me, let alone someone I haven't done a background check on.

So I'd be staying at Camelback Hotel, since falling lights, cut-up pillows, and tampered elevators were easier to handle than a stranger rubbing essential oils on my back.

"Do you need anything more from us?" I asked.

Detective Bunny shook her head, and from the pink in her cheeks, I'm pretty sure she'd been staring at my chest again.

I resisted the urge to cross my arms. "Well, thank you," I said when all Rick did was leave. Apparently he took being trapped in an elevator personally.

I trailed a little behind Rick as he followed signs to get back to the public part of the hotel. He hesitated in the lobby before turning in the the opposite direction of the elevators and disappearing through the door marked STAIRS. I froze. While I didn't want to get back in an elevator anytime soon, I also didn't want to walk up seven floors to get to Darren's room.

Just then the screech of a luggage cart reminded me just how bad my headache was.

Coffee first.

It's not like I'm proud of myself for walking shirtless through a pseudo-fancy hotel lobby to get a cup of free coffee. But seeing as I'd been up since six and hadn't had a drop of caffeine, people looking at me funny was the least of my problems.

The coffee was a little hotter than was comfortable to chug, but I drank the whole cup without taking a break to breathe. After refilling the cup, I started walking toward the stairs. I didn't notice Juniper until she was standing directly in front of me.

"Where have you been?" she asked, her arms crossed and her hip popped. "It's time for you to break up."

CHAPTER 13

B reak up?

My jaw tightened. "We're really doing this?"

Juniper stuck her finger in my face. "Your assistant is an obsessed stalker-killer, and I'm going to prove it."

"Whatever."

It had taken one and a half cups of coffee, but I now noticed the majority of people in the lobby wore conference badges. Checking my phone, I saw it was 9:57 a.m. I almost wished the elevator had been stuck for another twenty minutes so I'd be spared this charade.

"Where is she?" I asked.

"Outside." Juniper tilted her head toward the exit. "We went up to Darren's, but he said you were stuck or something..." For the first time my sister seemed to actually notice I was bare-chested. She just shook her head, like me being dressed inappropriately was a regular occurrence.

"I can explain," I said.

But Juniper shook her head. "We don't have time. You have to go."

Fine.

I spotted Brittany on the other side of a floor-to-ceiling window. A new sense of dread filled my stomach as I walked outside.

"Holt!" Brittany's eyes were wide as she took in my disheveled appearance. "What happened?"

I shrugged. "Check your voicemail, or I'll tell you later." I looked Britt straight in the eye. "Are we really doing this?"

"But..." Britt hesitated, clearly wanting to know why I was wandering around a hotel in nothing but my badge and dress pants.

"Come on," I said. "I'm supposed to get on a tour bus any minute."

"Right." Britt tucked a strand of hair behind her ear before her eyes shyly met mine. "Um, yeah, we're doing this."

I squeezed my eyes shut. I never wanted to break up with Britt—even if it was make-believe. "Okay," I practically whispered. When I reopened my eyes, they were cold and my jaw was tensed. "I can't believe you." My voice came out as more of a growl.

For a moment confusion and horror played across my girlfriend's face. I winked to make sure she knew I was just playing my part.

"You're the one who's impossible!" Brittany's voice was unnaturally shrill, and the way she was flapping her arms was...over the top.

I clenched my fists, channeling all of today's frustration. "I'm not the one who doesn't trust their boyfriend enough to go on a four-day business trip alone."

Whoa. Surprise flashed in both our eyes, and I hoped Britt could see I didn't really think that. All those teen movies were right. You should script a fake breakup.

"You know what"—Britt had on a sickening smile—"do whatever you want *without* me."

"Oh, so we're finally done?" I asked, trying to sound as nasty as I could.

"Yeah. We're done." And Britt began to walk away.

I gulped. Fake or not, it felt wrong to have her storm off. A voice an awful lot like Juniper's whispered in my head, *Stick to the plan, Holt.*

I was halfway through the hotel's entrance when I was struck with a moment of inspiration. Turning around, I yelled at Britt's back,

"That's great. I'll just date someone else." Now for the magnum opus. "You know sooner or later all women fall in love with me."

There were gasps and whispers from the lobby as people reacted to my final arrogant line.

Britt's shoulders stiffened, and she turned around slowly until she was facing me.

Had I gone too far?

But her eyes were dancing and her lips quivered like it was all she could do to keep from laughing. We stared at each other for a moment. She managed to say, "Congratulations." Then she left.

I know it was all pretend. Still, I felt something hard and painful settle in my chest as she walked away. With that, I entered the hotel and marched toward the stairwell.

"Wait!" Gabby was a little breathless as she sort of jogged in heels to catch up with me.

Was Gabby racing through the lobby ten seconds after my breakup to admit she loved me? I blame the lack of caffeine, but for a horrifying moment I was afraid Juniper was right.

"You have a bus to get on."

The bus?

I didn't try to stop my groan. "Gabby, I've been stuck in a roasting elevator for hours, I lost my shirt, have drunk barely any coffee, and my girlfriend just dumped—or I just dumped my girlfriend. Tell them I have food poisoning."

"I'm really sorry. But that's not going to work." Gabby moved to block the entrance to the stairs. "It doesn't matter what happened. You missed the CEO's breakfast, and I keep being asked if you'll *at least* be golfing and I've assured all of them that you will." I opened my mouth to argue, but Gabby held up her hand. "I'll get you a shirt and more coffee. Later we can figure something out about Brittany. I promise."

Weird.

What exactly did Gabby plan on *figuring out* about Brittany?

"Just sit down and I'll take care of it," Gabby said. She left without waiting to see what I did.

I sat.

Not because I believed Gabby would somehow save the day but because if I slunk off to mope, Gabby would find me and do whatever it took to get me on the bus—even if she had to drag me by the ear.

Across the room, Juniper sent a thumbs-up. She probably assumed Gabby had been confessing her undying love when she'd run to catch me. I shook my head. Sometimes Juniper is impossible to deal with...At least we no longer lived together.

Someone from the conference was halfway through explaining guidelines for our outing when Gabby returned with a small bag from what I can only assume was a hotel gift shop—though I hadn't noticed a gift shop in the hotel.

"Here's a can of Starbucks double shot," Gabby said. "I didn't think you had your sunglasses, so I got you a pair. And the shirt...well...I got the best—or only—option they had."

At first I was too distracted by the cheap aviators Gabby had handed me to check the T-shirt she was holding.

But when I looked...

"No." I stood up. "Absolutely not."

The shirt Gabby was handing me was pale yellow. I unfolded it and discovered the shirt was way worse than I'd imagined. Not only was it tiny, but some designer had used cheap-looking graphics to write *Phoenix* with a dumpy little cactus to one side sitting in a neon orange pot.

"Gabby?"

She shook her head. "That's all they had. Just put the shirt on. People are already getting on the buses."

For a moment I couldn't move, just kept staring down at the shirt. Was I really about to wear this abomination in front of my colleagues?

"Holt," Gabby said.

Whatever.

I slid the shirt on. It was tight around my neck and armpits, but I somehow wriggled into it. The fabric was so light and stretched out, the outline of my abs and belly button was obvious. Somehow this shirt was worse than being bare-chested.

"What size is this?"

"Small." Before I could protest, Gabby added, "They only had small. Now get on a bus."

I squeezed my eyes shut and tried to calm down. I hadn't been looking forward to today, and the reality was much worse than I'd imagined.

Gabby was still hovering, and if I didn't get on a bus soon, she'd step up her tactics. I left the hotel and got on a bus, keeping one hand on my shirt to keep it from becoming a midriff. At first I was relieved that I was on the same bus as Darren. Unfortunately, the two execs who'd obsessed over me all weekend were also on the bus. Before I could sit beside Darren, Female Exec had taken me by the arm. "We saved you a seat," she said before forcing me into the middle seat.

It was pretty rude. Nobody who is six foot one should ever have to sit in a middle seat.

"Quite the morning you had," Male Exec said—loudly *not asking* about the slacks paired with a skintight T-shirt when everyone else was dressed for golfing.

Since all he'd said was a statement, I nodded and began drinking my double shot of espresso.

Before either of them could ask me any questions, I decided to ask mine.

"For your retirement presentation, had you ever done that bit with the bubbles before?" In the elevator, it had been bugging me who knew the bottles of bubbles would be used. Were the two execs the only people?

"Oh." Female Exec's face lit up. "I thought of that over New Year's. It really gets the point across, right?"

I made a noncommittal sound in the back of my throat.

Male Exec seemed to guess what I was really asking. "This was the first time we did the bubble trick. We broke the seals off the first night, when we were setting up."

That meant my bottle of fake blood was tampered with in Arizona.

"Were people around as you set up?"

The Female Exec leaned over so she could look at the Male Exec.

"Maybe," he said.

"We went to the Sun Room after the police took our statements. We were both interviewed and cleared early on, since we had to rehearse our program," Female Exec said.

Hold on. They'd used their sway as VPs to be interviewed early? I was this year's golden boy. Why hadn't I gotten special treatment? I'd been stuck on that terrace for hours.

Female Exec hummed to herself. "There were some people around for random setup, but I don't remember who."

Unfortunately, my list of People Who Want Holt Dead wasn't growing any shorter with my current hunch.

I fell silent, which was a mistake since it gave my new fans a chance to ask me stuff.

"We missed you at breakfast. Were you really stuck in an elevator that whole time?" Male Exec asked.

I nodded.

"Were you terrified?" Female Exec asked. "I'm sure if I was stuck in an elevator I would be terrified."

"No, but—" I'd been about to say *But Rick was panicking*. Probably best to keep that detail private, given Rick's professional career was already on shaky ground.

"Do *you* know how it happened?" Female Exec asked.

Granted, I might not be thinking clearly given I was undercaffeinated and wearing a tacky yellow shirt that pinched my armpits and a pair of four-dollar aviators, yet the way she asked *do you know* made me wonder if she could be involved.

"The detective in charge gave me an update," I said vaguely.

"I see." She sat back, clearly disappointed I wasn't ready to gossip.

While either one of them from time to time tried to start up a conversation, I was in no mood to give anything but one-sentence answers, and Rick wasn't around to *encourage* my participation.

Come to think of it, where was Rick? I hadn't noticed him on our bus, but he could easily have gotten on a different bus.

It would have been nice to rest my eyes on the drive, but unfortunately I was sandwiched between two directors at BECKS. It was already bad enough that I hadn't brushed my teeth or showered after sweating profusely in the elevator. I definitely wasn't going to wake up drooling and sprawled across the lap of a high-ranking executive.

I did my best to stay alert, but I was dozing when the bus stopped at the golf course—Darren would say I needed to be more aware of my surroundings given someone wanted me dead.

It took at least five minutes, but felt more like ten, for everyone to leave the buses and form a large group. A lot of additional instructions were given, but I didn't pay attention. I was standing next to Darren, and he'd tell me the important parts.

"Let's go," Darren said when the voice with the loudspeaker finally shut up.

There were rows of tables with names printed out on badges with the golf course logo in the upper-right-hand corner. Darren moved off to the last table since his last name was Woods. I stayed back. There were too many people crowding around, pawing grubby hands over all the badges. No way was I going to wade into that chaos. Best to wait until the crowd had thinned out.

Suddenly Gabby was at my side. "Here." She handed over my golf course badge.

"Thanks," I said, clipping it to the front of my conference badge.

She gave a professional smile. "It was close to mine."

Really?

For a second I tried to remember her last name. Then I took the easy way out and read her full name off her badge. My hunch had been correct. Gabby's last name was Benson, which wouldn't be anywhere near Jacobs.

She'd lied about the badges being close. Which meant, either my sister was right and Gabby was in love with me, or she was just a really good assistant.

"We'll need to find Darren," Gabby said.

"Why?"

Gabby flipped her golf ID to show the backside of the name tag. Printed on that side were a number twelve and four names: Gabby Benson, Holt Jacobs, Rick Olson, Darren Woods.

Probably if I'd listened to the instructions, I'd already know this meant we were all on a team.

"There he is."

I followed Gabby's gaze to where Darren was walking toward us with a million-dollar smile. When he reached us, Darren gave me a quick clap on the back. "I thought they'd separate us."

Before I could answer, Gabby said, "Let's go," and started walking to the twin golf carts with the number twelve on each hood.

"What about Rick?" I asked, a few steps behind her.

"Rick stayed at the hotel."

I frowned. "Isn't this mandatory?"

"Yes." Gabby paused so I could catch up. "But Rick was stuck in an elevator for a few hours."

What?

"Hold on." It took effort for me not to raise my voice. "I was stuck in the same elevator, and you made me get on the bus."

"That's true."

"Are you kidding me?" My voice was extra deep in an overcorrection to keep from yelling.

Gabby sighed. "Look, all I know is Rick called to say he was skipping golf, but I had to make sure you showed up."

"Unbelievable."

We'd reached the golf carts, which were preloaded with clubs, and Darren had taken the driver's seat of one cart, but I hung back with Gabby, not quite ready to let the subject drop. I'm pretty sure Rick insisting I attend the golf event was just Rick being Rick, but what if he was the one trying to kill me and he'd planned something out on the course?

"What else did he say?"

Gabby looked at me curiously. "Nothing."

What did that look mean? Then I remembered my little breakup and tried to add heartbroken to my face, which was already wrinkled up in frustration.

"Well, I bet Rick didn't get dumped this morning. From where I'm standing, his day's better than mine."

"But Rick—" Gabby started to say when Male Exec walked up.

"Glad I caught you."

At his arrival, Darren left the cart and came to stand beside me and Gabby.

Since Gabby and Darren didn't speak, I said, "Yeah, we're here. Did you need something?"

The man straightened. "I'm your fourth."

"Okay" is what I said, but I was trying to figure out why Male Exec would join us when he'd presumably been assigned to another group of four.

Apparently my response may have come across as rude, because Darren extended his hand and said, "Welcome aboard, Drew. Here, why don't you ride with me?"

I glared at Darren for banishing me to the second cart, but he widened his eyes and tilted his head toward Gabby.

Ugh. Time to find out if my shared assistant had developed a secret crush after our months of working together—a theory that was utterly absurd.

As we loaded up, Darren started telling Male Exec about his first day at the company. Darren had gotten lost in the building and ended up trapped in a stairwell with a deactivated ID.

It was an amusing enough story but one I'd heard Darren tell too many times.

The story was half-over when Darren began driving the cart. I followed close behind. The cart dipped on an uneven patch. "Sorry," I muttered.

Gabby didn't seem to hear me. She was looking off into the distance while subconsciously biting her lip.

I tried to get better settled in the driver's seat. Gabby didn't seem in any mood to talk, and I wasn't going to ask if she loved me. Darren led the way past multiple tee offs, presumably leading us to the twelfth hole.

My mind wandered back to Brittany. I really wanted to call her and find out how she was after the fake fight. The problem with being pretend dumped is it would be pretty suspicious if we started chatting on the phone.

I was lost in my own thoughts and was surprised when Gabby's hand suddenly gripped my forearm.

"Why exactly did you and Brittany break up?"

CHAPTER 14

W ow.

Instinctively, I wanted to get Gabby's hand off my arm and tell her to mind her own business. Problem was, the whole point of the pretend breakup was to get Gabby talking. Then again, I should behave like usual so Gabby wasn't suspicious...How did I balance the two?

Trying to find the middle ground, I eased my arm out of Gabby's grasp and decided to say something vague. "It's complicated."

"But you're really broken up?"

Could Gabby tell the fight was staged?

"Um, yeah." My voice went quiet. "We're really broken up."

I swallowed hard. Was this really happening? Would Gabby grab my hands and declare her undying love?

There was a moment of hesitation in Gabby's eyes, and then they hardened with resolve. I gripped the golf cart, ready for the inevitable.

"You need to fix it," she said.

My jaw relaxed, and suddenly my mouth was hanging open. "Excuse me?" I asked.

"You need to apologize, or beg, or do whatever's necessary to get Brittany back."

It was work to stop my grin. Juniper was positive Gabby had a murderous crush on me, and here Gabby was insisting I fix things with my girlfriend.

I managed to sound serious when I asked, "And how is my personal life any of your business?"

Pink crept up Gabby's neck, but her perfect posture remained. "I have to work with you every day."

What was that supposed to mean?

The blush continued up into her cheeks, but Gabby kept talking. "I didn't work as closely with you until this year, but the whole floor knew when you met Brittany."

I ran a self-conscious hand through my hair. Given all the misadventures, national news, and sick days I'd had to take because of the trip to Oregon where I'd met Britt, it wasn't exactly a shock I'd been the main topic of office gossip.

As if reading my mind, Gabby shook her head. "That's not what I meant."

"Then what?" I asked—kind of hoping she wouldn't answer.

"Before last May, most people at work hadn't seen you smile. And after that, I don't know...it's like you relaxed. You were more open to thinking through other people's suggestions. And I'm sure Brittany's the reason you had your breakthrough."

My jaw twitched. Could that be right? My breakthrough was definitely with the help of the fairly talented members of my team. But the actual moment everything fell into place, I was with Britt. We'd been flying back from my family's Christmas in Montana. I had an aisle seat and was doodling equations while my free hand held hers. Then, unexpectedly, months of work clicked into place.

My throat sort of clogged—probably allergies from the Arizona golf course. When I spoke, my voice didn't sound right. "The reason I was acting different after Oregon was because of a brain injury. It had nothing to do with Britt."

I don't know why I said it. Even if we were truly broken up, it was a nasty thing to say. Gabby opened her mouth, then shut it again, and we rode the rest of the way in silence.

———————❦———————

"How are things working out with Gabby?" Male Exec asked partway through our first hole.

"Um…" What was he talking about? Surely he didn't think I was having an inappropriate relationship with my assistant.

"Isn't she helping with your scheduling and presentations?"

"Right. Yeah." Of course that's what he meant. "Uh, she's great."

We'd been walking a little behind Darren and Gabby, but he still lowered his voice. "Everyone on the board really appreciates how you've stepped up the past few weeks."

Stepped up? I hadn't *stepped up* to anything. Sure, I was working the occasional extra hour or two and my responsibilities had shifted, but everything I was doing remained in my job description.

"You know Rick's a wonderful man, but he's getting up in years."

Yikes. Was he about to offer me Rick's job? This couldn't be happening. Before he could make an offer, I decided to be a butt. "Isn't Rick in his fifties?"

Male Exec seemed to momentarily choke on air. "Could be. Could be. But as I was saying—"

"Heads!" a voice yelled.

My instincts from playing Little League had me crouched and protecting my head.

"What is—" Male Exec began asking as a golf ball whizzed past. It missed him, but if I hadn't ducked, the full force would have hit the back of my head.

Hearing the commotion, Darren and Gabby rejoined us just as a young guy came running up.

"My bad," he said.

One look at the guy and it was clear he wasn't in league with my wannabe-murderer. He was all muscle with no coordination...and there was a chance he wasn't old enough to get into bars.

Darren's mouth was pressed in a line. I'm pretty sure he was fighting his protective instincts to keep from going full lawyer on the guy.

Male Exec gave what was probably intended as a *fatherly* smile. "No harm done. Who else is in your group?"

The guy rattled off a list of three names.

Male Exec nodded—like he knew what face belonged to what name. "Dobson's a good enough golfer. Listen to him and you shouldn't decapitate anyone today."

The guy's ears turned a bright red, but he said, "Yes, sir," and left with his ball.

Darren let out a low whistle while the guy was still in earshot. "He's never held club before." None of us replied to Darren's comment, and Gabby began shooing us down the green to keep the game going.

As Darren got back into his golf cart, I practically dove to sit beside him. I couldn't ride in a cart with Gabby telling me how awesome Britt was. And no way was I riding with Male Exec. I wasn't going to suffer through more conversations about Rick being *too old*. And I didn't need to hear that I was the perfect genius they'd been waiting for.

Darren gave my arm a shove. "That's Drew's spot."

"It's okay," Male Exec said. "I'll drive the other cart."

Darren didn't wait for Gabby and Male Exec to get in their cart before he sped off. "Has Gabby talked to you?" There was an extra edge to his voice.

"She mentioned the breakup," I said, taking the chance to rest my eyes.

"And?"

And? I peeked an eye open. Darren was trying to sound casual, but his whole body was tense.

"You like her!" I said, sitting up.

"Who?"

Darren playing dumb was beneath him.

I shook my head. "You like Gabby."

Why hadn't I put it together before? Darren was so sure Gabby didn't have a secret crush on me because he had a secret crush on her.

"How long have you liked her?"

Darren didn't say anything, just stared straight ahead with his jaw locked.

Whoa. Darren *really* liked her.

I didn't say anything else. When we reached a spot near our golf balls, Darren stopped but didn't immediately get out of the cart. While he'd dated plenty in the time we'd been friends, there had never been a girl who made him nervous. What was it about Gabby? Was he attracted to her extreme organizational skills?

I think Darren had meant to say something, but he let the silence stretch for so long that Male Exec and Gabby had driven up.

I considered saying something mature, but where's the fun in that? Instead I murmured as I got out of the golf cart, "Don't worry. I'll put in a good word for you."

Darren's eyes bulged and he opened his mouth to reply, but no sound came out.

The other two were waiting. "Shall we?" I asked with a wink—not that he saw the wink since I was wearing the cheap shades Gabby had gotten me from the gift shop.

The following three holes were uneventful. Darren worked hard to avoid me and Gabby, which meant he was making small talk with Male Exec. It worked for me, I really didn't want Male Exec finishing a conversation that started with *you know Rick's old*.

Then came the sixteenth hole. Male Exec was well ahead, while Darren, Gabby, and I had similar scores. If it were just me and Darren playing, we'd get pretty competitive, but given the company and the personal black clouds hanging over us, we were more or less playing on autopilot.

But at the start of the sixteenth hole, Darren hit his ball straight into a sand trap. Male Exec laughed and said, "I thought you'd played golf before."

I'd been getting ready to tee off, but I froze at his comment, and my head snapped to Darren. I know it was one of those rude comments that you're just supposed to laugh off. Usually, my instincts would lead me down the nonconfrontational path, but I was undercaffeinated.

"Darren?" My voice was so low only he heard.

Darren shook his head. Apparently, I was expected to behave myself. Instead of an outburst, I set the ball on my tee and hit it with all my anger.

I lost track of the ball as I felt fabric ripping under my right arm, followed by a breeze on bare skin.

Worst shirt ever.

Darren's chuckle, which he tried to turn into a cough, reminded me that other people were around. Running a hand through my hair, I tried to hide some of my annoyance before I faced everyone with a massive tear in my already atrocious skintight shirt.

Gabby covered her mouth and stared down at the grass. She was probably half a second away from bursting into laughter.

"Well…" Male Exec said, but he seemed at a loss for words. Then he began a slow clap. "Congratulations, Holt. I had no idea you could hit a hole in one."

I'd done what now?

"Um…" Checking the course, I tried to spot my ball but couldn't. "Thanks."

I raised an eyebrow at Darren, but he shrugged—all he'd noticed was my shirt ripping. Ordinarily, I would have been excited about my first hole in one, but ordinarily I'm not at a work conference wearing something that resembles a bro-tank.

"You two go ahead," Male Exec was saying to Darren and Gabby. "You'll be up next anyway."

I don't know if Darren had always been so stiff around Gabby or if it was heightened because he was uncomfortable I'd figured it out. Whatever the reason, he gave a strange sort of half bow to Gabby before saying, "After you."

They drove off, leaving me alone with the exec.

Male Exec got into the driver's seat of the second golf cart, but he wasn't in a hurry to leave.

I needed to be clear with him. I wasn't interested in taking over for Rick. No way did I want to start being in charge of people. Overseeing squabbles and approving vacation time really wasn't my style.

"Look—" I wanted to say Male Exec's name but couldn't remember it. Glancing at his name tag, I saw DREW MACINTIRE. "Look, Drew, about Rick—"

But Male Exec interrupted me. "It's a shame about your shirt. Did you watch the movie?"

Movie?

"Uh...no."

"I just dated myself."

"Sure," I said. For all his talk of Rick being *old*, Male Exec had to be around Rick's age.

"Anyway, that shirt is iconic."

"Yellow with a cactus?" I couldn't keep the skepticism out of my voice.

"Yeah..." Male Exec squinted up toward the sky. "I guess you'd need to watch the movie to get it."

I sincerely doubt watching the film would help me *get anything* about the tacky yellow shirt.

"Was that from the hotel gift shop?" he asked.

I nodded.

"Did they also sell the Desert Sands shirt?"

Was he still talking about the movie? "Uh, I don't think so. Gabby said this was all they had."

"Too bad. I'd buy a Desert Sands shirt if they had them. It was this local bar where the final showdown happened."

I managed to sound serious as I said, "Cool."

Male Exec began to drive, and we rode together in silence. Just when I thought we were too close to the others for Male Exec to bring up my replacing Rick, he said, "I understand you're not ready to discuss your future, but let me know when you are ready." Then he handed me a card and walked off.

While Male Exec tried to be nonchalant, Darren and Gabby had definitely noticed—though they acted like they weren't watching.

I raised my hand in a half wave and heard my shirt rip even more.

"Here," Darren said, taking off his pale pink polo to fully show off his huge biceps in a white tank top.

I frowned. "You showing off for your girlfriend?"

Darren's nostrils flared, but he didn't take the bait.

I ripped off the yellow tee and put on his slightly damp polo. "Thanks," I muttered.

Instead of answering, Darren crowded into my personal space. "Does Drew giving you his card mean what I think it means?"

I checked to make sure Gabby was out of earshot before saying, "Yeah, it does."

"What are you going to do?" Darren asked.

I shook my head. "I don't want Rick's job."

"Does Rick know?"

I met Darren's eyes. Suddenly Rick was a suspect again.

CHAPTER 15

I snagged a seat next to Darren on the bus ride back to the hotel. As much as I wanted to take a nap, there was lots to do and not a lot of time to do it all.

I texted Britt, asking her to meet us at the Camelback Hotel with Juniper.

Britt: *Aren't we broken up?*

Two seconds later she sent a winkie face.

It was official. My girlfriend had spent too much time with my sister. Still, I came up with a pretty good reply.

Me: *We can still be friends.*

Apparently Britt agreed I'd nailed my reply, because she sent a GIF of a little kid doing a spit take, followed by a GIF of a judge from a singing competition giving a standing ovation.

Before I'd locked my screen, the phone lit up with a new text from Mom: *I'm waiting.*

I slumped against my seat. It wasn't enough that I was juggling being the conference golden boy, a fake breakup, and surviving a killer stalker, but I also needed to find the right words to get Mom off my back.

I scrubbed a hand against my jaw. I could do this. One disaster at a time.

What with being busy at the conference and the time difference between Arizona and Australia, I'd successfully ignored and forgotten Mom for more than twenty-four hours.

What could I say?

Me: *Sorry. The conference has been wild. I'll call tomorrow from the airport.*

After pressing send, I held my breath. If Mom agreed, I'd either miss the call because my wannabe killer had succeeded, or I'd need to explain over the phone all of my misadventures in a crowded airport. Neither option was ideal.

When Mom did reply, it was only one word, but it was all I needed.

Mom: *Okay.*

As far as parental oversight was concerned, I'd been granted a stay of execution.

Once we returned to the hotel, I headed straight to Darren's room to brush my teeth and take a shower. I risked an elevator ride since I didn't want to walk up seven flights of stairs in my dress shoes. Suspiciously, Darren hung back to chat with Gabby.

Not to make it all about me, but it would be kind of weird if my best friend started dating my assistant. It's not like they'd talk about me the whole time...but I'd definitely come up.

The shower was the best thing to happen to me all day. Not only had I sweated a lot in the elevator, but I'd also golfed eighteen holes. I felt so much better after. Instead of changing straight into my suit for the evening's closing presentations, I put on one of the hotel's bathrobes—really comfortable if you ignored how many naked strangers had previously worn it.

When I came out of the bathroom, Britt was sitting on my bed, Juniper was perched on the table with Chouzie at her feet, while Darren had the room's office chair.

"Don't worry," Juniper said before I'd fully exited the bathroom. "We wore disguises so no one would be suspicious that Brittany was back after the two of you broke up."

Had Juniper disguised her chow chow? Since I was afraid of her answer, I didn't ask. Instead I commented, "Disguises weren't necessary."

"Gabby *didn't* talk to you about the breakup?"

My jaw ticked. "Oh, she talked about it."

Juniper clapped. "I knew she had a thing for you."

"Nooo." I sat next to Brittany and took her hand. "Gabby told me I should beg and grovel so Brittany would take me back. Because..." I sighed. "Because she's the best thing that's ever happened to me."

Britt squeezed my hand. "Sounds about right."

"Whatever," I said, but I was grinning.

"Gross." Juniper began tapping on her phone. "Please say there was another reason for calling this meeting beyond making googly eyes at your girlfriend."

"Oh, there was." I stretched my legs out to get more comfortable. "First, there was the pleasure of telling you that you were wrong about Gabby."

Juniper arched an eyebrow. "You don't find her attractive?"

"What...? I...no, er..."

Juniper was positively trembling with glee, Chouzie yelped his approval, and Britt let go of my hand—not what I wanted.

I cleared my throat. "As I was saying, we've crossed *tortured love* off the list of reasons for murder. That leaves someone who either blames me for shutting down the South Dakota factory, or Rick doesn't want me stealing his job."

Darren had been staring blankly at the wall, but at that he blinked. "Isn't Rick the obvious suspect?"

"Well..." I shook my head. Not only did I hope he wouldn't kill me due to all the years we'd worked together, but there was no faking the panic he'd experienced when we'd been trapped in the elevator. Also, according to Detective Bunny, the elevator had been tampered with. It was likely related to the other mishaps. Rick couldn't be in the elevator and in the control room at the same time.

"So," Britt said, twining her fingers between mine. "Our options are revenge for destroying a small town's commerce or removing you from Rick's succession line."

"Who'd get Rick's job if you weren't in the way?" Juniper asked.

"Darren," I said.

Britt gasped, and Juniper nearly dropped her phone.

Darren shook his head, not at all amused. "He's lying. We're not even in the same department."

Britt swatted my shoulder, while Juniper stuck her tongue out.

"Hold on." Juniper had on her impish little-sister face. "I feel like we're ignoring the most likely option for wanting to kill Holt."

Darren made the mistake of asking, "Which is?"

Juniper said, "He's annoying," right as I said, "I'm annoying."

My sister's eyes widened.

I shrugged. "Your insults aren't very original."

"Well, your face..." Juniper trailed off.

"Getting back to the case," Britt said. "If the killer plans on getting Holt while he's in Phoenix, they're running out of time."

"Exactly," I said.

Darren tapped on the table. "It would be easiest to track the South Dakota angle. Juniper, why don't you internet stalk everyone who's been spending an abnormal amount of time around Holt."

"Yes, sir," Juniper said with a cheesy salute. "Who am I stalking?"

Suddenly all eyes were on me.

"Uhh...the two execs," I said.

Darren added, "That's Sasha Redding and Drew MacIntire."

"Then Rick—"

"Olson," Darren interrupted before I could say the last name.

"And Gabby—"

"Benson."

He would know Gabby's full name.

My phone lit up with a reminder from Gabby that the presentations would start in twenty minutes. "I need to change," I said. "Juniper, work fast on your internet stalking. We have twenty minutes."

"Really?" Darren jumped up. "I need to shower."

I ended up changing and doing my hair in the alcove by the bathroom sink while Darren showered. Hurrying, we were both ready with seven minutes to spare.

I'd put on my best suit and my most expensive pair of cuff links and had spent extra time on my hair. Tonight I was either giving a speech or I'd die trying. Whichever happened, I wanted to look my best.

"Ready?" I asked Britt and Juniper as I rounded the corner.

Juniper was immediately on her feet with Chouzie's leash and was heading for the door, but Brittany's eyes went wide. "Oh" was all she said.

She was staring at me. What was wrong? I fidgeted with my collar, trying to remember what I'd looked like in the mirror. Hadn't I looked good? It's not like there was spinach in my teeth. Then Britt's eyes softened, and a slow, intimate smile lit up her face.

"How do I look?" My voice was strangely husky.

My sister broke the moment by saying, "You look phenomenal." Then she grabbed my wrist and pulled me out of the room.

Britt and Darren followed. I kept sneaking glances at Brittany. I *really* wanted to kiss her, but Juniper had other ideas.

We were halfway to the elevator when Juniper stopped in her tracks. Since she had Chouzie's leash and was still holding on to me, we also stopped. Darren half crashed into me, while Britt managed to get out of the way.

"This isn't right," Juniper said.

I raised an eyebrow. "You'll have to be more specific."

"Brittany can't be hanging around since the two of you split up."

I half laughed. "You can't be serious."

Juniper's chin jutted up. "Of course I'm serious. The two of you just had a very public breakup. It'd be really suspicious if you're suddenly together again."

"We tried your scheme. Gabby wasn't jealous. It didn't work." Britt's eyes were bright with emotion. "I love Holt. I'm not going to hide in a hotel room while someone tries to kill him."

Juniper's nose scrunched. She's used to getting her way and didn't quite know how to respond. But everyone could tell, no matter what, Britt would refuse to leave my side.

My chest expanded. I didn't want her to leave.

This time I couldn't stop myself from kissing Britt. I broke free of Juniper's grasp. With one hand on Britt's hip pulling her close and the other in her hair, I kissed her like it was the final scene in a movie.

When we broke apart for air, Darren placed a firm hand on my shoulder. "Understood. Holt and Britt are no longer broken up."

I heard what Darren said, but I didn't really process the meaning. It was Britt whispering, "Your speech...We have to go," that had me loosening my grip on her and resuming the walk to the elevator.

Juniper's face had flushed a bright shade of red. It seemed she was really uncomfortable with me making public displays of affection right in front of her. Kind of hypocritical, given Juniper's made out with her husband in front of me numerous times.

It wasn't until we were waiting for an elevator that Darren asked. "Juniper, did you discover anything with your internet sleuthing?"

"Um, yeah…" Juniper still appeared flustered, but she tried to rally. "I did a quick deep dive on all our suspects. Nothing on Rick, Gabby, or Drew, but your other exec—uh, Sasha—she has a lot of photos with her son. He plays football for a team called…the Coyotes."

Coyotes? Was I expected to know what state that team was from?

"Are the Coyotes from South Dakota?" Britt was mature enough to ask.

"Give me a sec." Juniper tapped at her phone. The elevator doors dinged opened just as Juniper looked up from her phone. "Yes. The Coyotes are from South Dakota. Sasha Redding's son plays football in South Dakota."

It wasn't much to go on. Was this the proof that Female Exec wanted me dead?

———◦◦◦———

"Okay, so game plan," Darren said in the elevator—totally uncon-cerned about the mom also inside with her toddler. "We'll want to keep a close eye on Sasha, but most important is to never let Holt out of our sight. Holt goes through doors second. The only beverages he drinks are ones we've already drank from. He will never be alone. Got it?"

Darren's face was set like a warrior ready for battle. He looked so intense I felt bad for raising my hand. Still, there was one weak spot in his plan.

"What about my speech?"

"Your speech?" Darren repeated like he didn't understand the words.

"You're still doing that?" Juniper asked—a silly question since short of being dead or trapped in an elevator for the second time in one day, there was no getting out of it.

"I have to give it," I said. "I'll be the last of four people giving fifteen-minute showcases."

"No," Britt whispered, the little scar by her eyebrow very defined.

Darren was shaking his head. "There's a fifteen-minute window when you'll be alone on an empty stage?"

"There will be a packed auditorium watching." I tried not to sound worried.

Darren frowned. "That still leaves you vulnerable to being shot, or another falling stage light, or..."

"A crossbow," Juniper added. "This killer is probably an expert with a crossbow."

I frowned at Juniper. She could take my impending demise a little more seriously. When I caught her eye, she tossed her hair, seemingly unbothered by my current predicament.

The elevator doors opened on the ground floor, and the mom hurried through with her kid.

I was about to give Darren a hard time for scaring a mom when Juniper started giggling. "Did you see her face?"

Maybe it was the stress or Juniper's infectious personality, but I began cracking up.

We weren't too far into the lobby when Britt grabbed my arm and held me back. "I've got Holt," she said when Darren stopped. "You keep an eye out for Sasha."

Darren pressed his lips together, but he nodded and followed Juniper and Chouzie to the auditorium.

"I don't like this," Britt said so quietly I had to bend close to hear.

"You don't like my suit?" I asked, deciding to keep things light. "You should have said something before we came down." I winked, but there was no amusement in Britt's eyes.

"Please, tell me you're taking this seriously."

I couldn't answer her. This might be denial talking, but I found it hard to believe someone hated me enough to want me dead. Thinking back over the conference, what had happened? Some pillows were cut up and I'd been slipped a bottle of fake blood. Even stuck in the elevator, I wasn't in any real danger. If anything, those pranks were the actions of a kid having a temper tantrum.

Why had we assumed someone wanted me dead?

The crash of the stage light echoed in my head.

Mr. Speaker was dead. Either a crafty killer had manipulated an empty stage into a high-concept mousetrap or...

"Holt?" Britt's hands were cupping my face.

I stepped back, possibly muttering to myself.

"Holt!" Britt repeated.

"What if the stage light wasn't supposed to kill him?"

"But..." Britt's paramedic mask fell into place, removing any real emotion from her features—she thought I was crazy. "Detective Bunny confirmed the light was tampered with."

"I know. I know." I paced around Britt, trying to form my thoughts into words. "But what if it was an accident?"

"It *wasn't* an accident." Britt had graduated from her paramedic face to speaking slowly while overenunciating. "Remember what Detective Bunny said?"

I forced myself to take a deep breath before trying again. "I mean what if the light was just supposed to *fall* during my speech? It wasn't supposed to hit anyone. That guy had really bad luck standing there."

"I see." Britt's face remained impassive, but she seemed to truly be thinking through my theory. "So for the first few minutes of your speech, you'd be distracted with the flashing lights, and then the stage light would drop and the rest of the speech would be canceled. You would never publicly announce your idea."

"Exactly," I said.

"There you are," Gabby called, interrupting our conversation. She was partway down the hallway that led to the auditorium. "You're late. You shouldn't be late." Even in heels, Gabby glided swiftly across the room. She moved to stand behind me, then sheep-dogged me toward the hallway. Britt was more or less caught up in the tide.

"Relax, Gabby," I said, feeling a sudden need for more coffee. "I'm the final talk in the showcase. It's okay if I don't hear the first speech. It's not like I'd learn anything that Bernard has to say."

Gabby ignored my attitude when she answered. "You need to be set up with a mic, and Rick wanted to speak to you." Gabby kept us walking past the auditorium's main doors and toward the stage entrance Rick had brought me through. "And Brittany..." Gabby sized up my girlfriend. Somehow Britt communicated nonverbally that she'd have to be forcibly removed from my side. "And Brittany can come along. I'm so glad the two of you worked things out."

Even to my ears the words sounded fake, but Britt nodded and said, "Thanks. It was all a misunderstanding."

Once we'd gone through the stage doors and were back in the dim, narrow hallway, I glanced at Gabby. All of Juniper's suggestions about Gabby made me second-guess freely going with her to a dark, abandoned corner of the hotel. But I had Brittany, and from the set of Britt's jaw, she wasn't going to let anything bad happen.

Maybe that's why I wasn't as worried as I should've been. I trusted the people in my life—though I could never tell them that.

Gabby brought us to a narrow door, and when neither Britt nor I turned the handle, she moved between us and opened the door.

My imagination had gotten the better of me. The interior wasn't some elaborate murder dungeon. Instead, it was a modest-sized dressing room, with lights around the mirror blazing brightly. Rick sat in the room's only chair, while a hotel employee stood by the wall with a lapel mic.

"Holt." Rick half stood at our entrance before sitting back on the chair.

Wordlessly, the hotel employee began touching me as he got the mic set up. Britt stood just inside the door, her face giving nothing away—she actually looked like a bodyguard. Gabby said something about checking on the showcase before leaving.

I'm not one for tracking the *energy* in rooms, but there were a lot of emotions held in the small space.

Rick rubbed a hand across his jaw. Maybe this was from the excessively bright lights in the dressing room, but he looked older, with deep wrinkles etched in drooping skin.

He said, "I wanted to know—" He cut himself off, eyeing the hotel employee who was pinning a lapel mic to my chest. "I wanted to know how golf went."

Golf?

Since I didn't answer immediately, Brittany replied for me, which began a tedious conversation full of small talk as we waited for the hotel employee to leave.

In reality, it didn't take very long for the mic to be set up with some sort of battery pack clipped to my belt. Still, I wanted to yell from all the tension building in the room.

My shoulders relaxed when the employee finally said, "You're set," and left. I pretended to fix my hair in the mirror as I prepared myself for whatever Rick might say.

But instead of confessing some deep dark secret, Rick just sat there. Britt, too, stopped speaking. It was the three of us in an empty room, and the only sound was the ticking of a wall clock I hadn't noticed before.

Tick, tock. Tick, tock. Tick—

Truly annoying things. I don't know how people survived centuries without digital clocks.

Also, fun fact, I'd kind of forgotten I had to give a speech. Did I have my notes? Shoving my hands in the different pockets of my suit, I came up empty. They must be in Darren's room.

I needed my notes.

It's not that I get stage fright...because I definitely *don't* get that. But starting in school and continuing through adulthood, if I ever had to talk in front of more than ten people, it wasn't uncommon for there to be a moment when my brain went blank. I couldn't remember what I'd been talking about, let alone what I was supposed to say next.

That's why I needed notes. In case my brain went blank, those little note cards kept me on track.

"Excuse me," I said, and from the strangled sound of my voice, I wondered if Rick and Britt thought I was about to vomit.

I flung the dressing room door open and was met with a wave of fresh air. I could do this. I could get my notes, give a speech, and not be murdered.

Everything was under control.

CHAPTER 16

B ritt followed. Of course Britt followed. If I'd given her a moment's thought, I'd have known she'd taken Darren's warning to heart and would never let me out of her sight.

"What's the matter?" she asked, running to catch up.

"I forgot my notes," I said as we made it into the lobby. I turned to look at Brittany, and just past her shoulder was the sign for the hotel's gift shop. That's where it was.

"Are you sure you want to go through with this?" Britt asked, but from the worry on her face, she already knew the answer.

All I could say was "Britt..." It wasn't like I enjoyed causing her worry, but this close to my speech I'd made a startling discovery—I actually wanted to give the presentation. It might be blockheaded, but this was my discovery, and this was my moment to explain it to my peers. I couldn't have a murderer and saboteur take that away from me.

It wasn't like I believed all the hype the execs were throwing at me. Still, what I'd accomplished was kind of a big deal.

We waited by the elevators with a group of people who looked (and smelled) like they'd spent the entire day hiking.

I turned to face away from them. Would the scent of sweat and dirt be overpowering in the elevator?

"No!" a man's voice cried out. It didn't take long to spot the guy in the lobby. He had one of those extra-large plastic soda cups with the liquid fizzing over, and half of his jersey was stained a light brown.

"Just wear it," his buddy was saying. "We're going to miss the game."

"Give me a second."

"There isn't time to go back to the room."

"I know." The spilled-drink guy sounded annoyed as he walked to the gift shop. He was about to be more annoyed when he discovered his only clothing option was a size small yellow shirt.

"You coming?" Britt's voice pulled me back to the problem at hand. She was now inside the elevator with the hikers.

Right.

I inhaled deeply before getting in. I'd be holding my breath as long as possible. It's not that the hikers smelled atrocious—but elevators are small.

Britt and I got to the room, I retrieved my notes, and we were back in the lobby in record time. We were so fast, the spilled-drink guy was just leaving the store with a small shopping bag. He appeared less irritated than when he'd spilled the drink. Granted, his buddy was hustling him out of the hotel, so I didn't get a good look. Still, if a small shirt was tight on me, I'm not sure how he'd be able to slither into it.

"Hurry," Britt called ahead of me.

I sped up and couldn't help grinning. Even though she didn't want me to take the risk of giving the speech, she was making sure I didn't miss it because it was important to me. I almost shouted *I love you* across the room. Since it was a public setting, I didn't proclaim my love. But I'd considered it, which shows just how crazy I was about Britt.

We made it down the hallway, and I was about to open the stage door when it was flung open.

"There you are," Gabby said. "Come on, you're being introduced."

I followed Gabby, somehow needing to jog as she glided across the backstage in her high heels. "It hasn't been forty-five minutes."

"Reese ran short."

"How short?"

But Gabby had disappeared through a curtain. I followed and ended up getting tangled before tearing myself free. I managed to stay silent, which was good because Gabby and I were now just offstage.

I turned back to give Britt a quick kiss, but she wasn't there.

"...no further introduction," Rick was saying, "Holt Jacobs."

There was applause, and as I started to walk back through the curtain to find my girlfriend, Gabby grabbed my arm and shoved me onstage.

I half tripped as the stage lights hit me, but I didn't care. Where was Britt?

Since I didn't keep walking to the podium, Rick moved to me and shook my hand before exiting the stage.

I swallowed.

Surely Britt was fine. But what if she wasn't? Should I go find her? As I stood debating, Britt appeared through the curtain and gave a little wave.

The knot in my stomach eased, and I walked to the podium.

I ran a hand through my hair and cracked a smile before making my voice bland and official. "The silver Buick with Colorado license plates has its lights on." There was a decent amount of polite laughter, and some of the tension in my forehead melted away.

I hadn't planned on telling a dumb joke, but what about this work retreat had gone as planned?

I took a deep breath, then delivered my speech. It actually went well. My mind never went blank, and I didn't need the note cards. Instead of being worried about falling stage lights or being struck in the heart with an arrow, I was fully present as I delivered my speech. It was pretty awesome—though not something I'd like to repeat anytime soon.

Once I'd made my final remark, the applause hit me and people began standing. For a second I froze, not knowing what I was supposed to do. Then I gave a little bow and exited.

Someone new took the stage and began introducing the evening's keynote speaker as my applause died down.

Britt was standing right offstage, and her eyes were bright. "Oh, Holt," she said, and I was crushing her in my arms and we were kissing. "I'm so proud of you," she whispered when we broke apart.

Before I could answer, Rick's hand was on my shoulder. "Go to your seats. There'll be plenty of time to celebrate once the seminar's over." Instead of looking happy or even pleased, his face was almost gray.

"Yes, sir."

I took Britt's hand, and we left the backstage to enter through the auditorium's main doors.

Juniper and Chouzie were standing by the entrance like they expected us. When Juniper saw me, she gave a little bounce on her toes and mouthed, *Wow*, and I think she was actually impressed. I couldn't stop grinning, and I winked at Juniper. My sister brought us to the row where Darren was sitting with three empty chairs beside him.

He gave me a quick thumbs-up before his attention returned to the keynote speaker. I sat with Darren on one side and Brittany on the other.

I wrapped my arm around Britt and pretended to listen, but my mind was worlds away.

This was the last scheduled event before the seminar wrapped up. Tomorrow we'd all be traveling back home. The good news, I was still alive, but the bad news was no arrests had been made. Would I be able to relax in my regular life always wondering if today was the day my attacker returned?

Was my theory correct that Mr. Speaker's death had been an accident? It hadn't been a scheme to lure me to a fatal spot during my speech. The flickering lights were meant as a distraction, not an over-the-top murder.

What did that really mean?

It made the South Dakota revenge option less likely. If you hated my guts for what I'd created, kill me or don't, but there's no benefit in toying with me.

Female Exec was sitting near the stage, and it seemed like the keynote speaker had her full attention. So what if her son played football in South Dakota. It in no way meant she'd take on a personal vendetta.

Applause started around me, and I joined in—not that I could comment intelligently on the speech's contents or delivery.

The event coordinator got onstage and made a few closing remarks, and then the audience lights were turned on and we were dismissed. I'd planned on disappearing in the crowd of faces exiting the auditorium, but I was surrounded by a sea of unknown people introducing themselves, shaking my hand, congratulating me, and asking questions. It was overwhelming.

Britt, Darren, and Juniper did what they could to deflect and answer for me as we slowly made it out of the auditorium, through the hallway, and into the lobby.

At this point, my fan club had thinned out enough that I could breathe again.

"Are you done?" Juniper asked.

"With the conference?" I asked.

"Uh-huh."

"Yeah, we're done," I said, not sure why she was asking.

"Great. There's this bar I found online. It has dancing. It'll be a fun place for us to celebrate."

I raised one of my eyebrows. *Dancing?* My sister expected me to go dancing?

"What about the case?" I asked.

"Eh." Juniper tossed her hair. "You're still alive, and who knows when we'll all be in Phoenix again. Let's have some fun."

"Maybe she's right," Britt said, but she didn't sound convinced.

"Holt." Darren's expression had the seriousness of a lawyer. "Do you think we'll solve this tonight?"

I tried not to squirm, but for some reason I felt like Darren was a teacher asking if I'd get my homework done in time.

"I mean...I hope I can." It wasn't a good answer, but I couldn't know if we'd solve the case. I was close to the truth. I knew I was close. But I couldn't say when—or if—all the pieces would fit together.

Darren nodded. He'd gone from lawyer to judge. "I'm with Juniper," he said. "Let's try to have some fun."

"We can trust Detective Bunny will do her job," Britt added.

They were all watching me, and from the look on Juniper's face, I could tell she wanted to say, *Don't be a butt.*

"Fine. Whatever. Let's go have fun."

Going to a bar sounded a lot like running away to me, but everyone else wanted to, and I didn't want to be the reason we all spent a night brooding over suspects in Darren's hotel room.

"Ah!" Juniper clapped her hands together. "Thanks, Holt." Then she flung her arms around me in a quick hug.

"Just don't expect me to dance," I whispered to Juniper.

Juniper giggled and said, "We'll see," as she stepped out of the hug.

We both knew I *could* dance. While in high school, my other sister, Casey, had pressured me into helping her practice swing dancing in our living room. Still, tonight wasn't the night to introduce Britt to that hidden talent.

Juniper's nose wrinkled as she did full-body scans of me and Darren. "You boys should change. Otherwise, people will think you're FBI agents surveilling the place."

"Ouch," Darren said. "You think my suit looks cheap?"

Juniper raised a finger. "I don't want to hear it. Go get ready. I'll step outside and do a quick livestream with Chouzie and then call my husband." With that my sister walked away—turning a few heads as she went.

"I'll stay down here," Britt said.

"You sure?" I asked.

"Yeah, I'll use the lobby bathroom. I'd just slow down the process if I went up."

"Okay."

Britt headed for the ladies' room, and Darren was already waiting for the elevator. I was about to join him when the gift shop sign struck something in my memory.

I closed my eyes, trying to figure out what my gut was trying to tell me. Gabby had gone there this morning. This evening there'd been the sports fan who'd spilled his drink. He'd bought a new shirt. I could see him carrying the bag. I squeezed my eyes even tighter.

Come on. What was it?

I blinked as my head snapped up. The bag was partly see-through, and a dark color had pressed against the side—nothing like the yellow shirt Gabby had made me wear.

Had Gabby said that shirt was the *best* option or the *only* option?

I nearly tripped over someone's suitcase in my hurry to get to the gift shop.

A shirt display was featured near the checkout. Not only were there larger sizes of the small yellow shirt Gabby made me wear, but there were also stacks of dark gray T-shirts with DESERT SANDS written across the chest.

Had Gabby been torturing me?

She knew that given the choice between gray or yellow, I'd go with gray. Also, no one would ever mistake my T-shirt size as small.

But I couldn't jump to conclusions. I had to do something dire—talk to the store clerk.

The shop's only cashier was busy checking out a customer, but once the transaction had wrapped up, the cashier batted her eyes and asked, "How can I help?"

My suit and exercise regime were definitely doing me favors in Phoenix.

I gave a polite nod while trying to imply, *I'm very committed to my girlfriend.* "Did you put more of these T-shirts on display this afternoon?"

"No." She was good enough at her job to act like I'd just asked a very normal question. "We've had these shirts out for the past month." She bent closer like she was telling a secret. "They haven't been selling much because the movie's so old, but today we sold two."

I nodded. "Um...thanks."

Then I left.

Gabby had gone to a display of shirts, and instead of picking a rather forgettable gray tee proclaiming DESERT SANDS, she'd not only chosen the tacky yellow option, but she'd chosen it in a size that was extremely tight on me.

That night on the terrace, Gabby had talked to Darren and me. Had Rick actually sent her over to tell me the CEO's breakfast was postponed? Had she used that opportunity to break into my hotel room and destroy the pillows? I'd like to think Darren or I would have recognized her, but it had been far away and I was too surprised by the intruder to take a good look.

Was I really so bad to work for that Gabby would make it her mission to ruin my trip? I'd been walking on autopilot but found myself back by the elevators. I pressed the *up* button, and for once the doors opened right away.

I got in, and as the doors closed, I tapped the seven.

"You didn't turn off your mic. It was still broadcasting in the sound booth. I heard all about your little T-shirt investigation."

My head rose slowly. I hadn't noticed anyone following me inside. Gabby was there, holding a large touristy knife with a decorated handle.

Darren was right. I should pay better attention to my surroundings.

CHAPTER 17

"Thank you, Gabby. That will be all," I said.

For a second the knife faltered, and Gabby's eyes clouded with confusion. The elevator had just passed the second floor. I pressed the three. If I could get out of the enclosed space, maybe I'd be all right.

But Gabby moved to block me from the doors with the knife pointed at me.

Interesting. I'm taller and bigger than Gabby. In a fight, I'd probably be able to take the knife away, but I'd rather not find out how much damage she could do before I took the knife. Besides, she was a single, former ballet dancer living in the city—she probably knew the kind of self-defense that'd leave me crying in the fetal position.

The elevator stopped, and the doors began opening. What if I charged her?

Then I heard voices on the other side—kids' voices.

Gabby's eyes went wide, and I held up my hands. "Truce?" Had I just said *Truce* like I was a fourth grader arguing over who got the last cookie?

"Truce," Gabby agreed, before moving to stand behind me. The hand with the knife slid under my blazer, and she rested the point at the area around my kidneys. Then she wrapped her free hand around my stomach.

When the door opened to a family of five, Gabby and I must've looked like a couple who couldn't take their hands off each other—not an assistant threatening her boss with a knife.

I forced something close to a smile. "Evening," I said.

"Evening," the dad said, carrying a cake box, while the mom helped the littlest kid press the button for the sixth floor.

"Babe?" At first I didn't realize Gabby was speaking to me—I'd never been her *babe*.

"What?" The pressure from the knife increased, that much closer to causing an injury. Time to play nice, so I added, "Sweetie."

Gabby's voice was overly sugary. "I was just thinking if you'd listened to your sister, we wouldn't be in this mess."

My body tensed. Was she serious?

I tried to keep my voice pleasant. "Sweetie, my sister wanted to go have fun at a bar, but I had to follow up on an idea."

"And you're known for your ideas." This time Gabby wasn't able to hide the bitterness. The mom glanced over before moving her kids close.

In all of my sister's wild theories about Gabby wanting me dead, she'd never pointed out that Gabby's time as a ballet dancer would make her comfortable in the backstage area of any theater. With her purposeful stride, no one would give her presence a second thought.

We didn't say anything else until the elevator stopped and the family left.

"Come on, Gabby," I said. "I know you didn't mean to kill anyone. What's your plan now?"

The pressure of the knife lessened. "I don't know." But just as quickly the pressure returned. "I didn't think you'd figure it out."

Before I could answer, the elevator stopped on the seventh floor.

"Don't try anything," Gabby said, accompanying the threat with cutting a hole through my shirt. Now the cold blade was touching my skin.

When the doors opened, Darren was standing in the hallway dressed in Hawaiian shorts and a polo. His eyebrows shot up at the sight of Gabby embracing me.

"Elevator's full," Gabby said.

I gave a slight shake of my head.

"I'll fit," Darren said. He got in, then asked, "Where are we headed?"

"Top floor," Gabby said.

Darren pressed the button for the top floor and stood in the diagonal corner facing us.

"Holt?"

I raised a shoulder, feeling a little safer with Darren there. "You're girlfriend's trying to kill me."

Pain momentarily flashed through Darren's eyes, but his voice was casual when he said, "She's not my girlfriend."

"What's going on?" Gabby asked, punctuating the question with a mini jab that didn't puncture skin.

"That's what I'd like to know," Darren said.

"Glad you asked," I said to Darren. "Gabby has a knife pressed against my kidneys."

"Sure," Darren said like that was normal.

"I'm still wearing the mic, and Gabby heard me figuring out that she was the one making my life...more complicated."

"That mic?" Darren asked.

"Uh-huh."

Our eyes met. Was someone else listening? Could help be on the way?

"Good idea," Gabby said. "But I turned off the mic before finding you."

Right. There was another irritating example of Gabby's attention to detail.

"Holt forgot about the mic and here we are?" Darren asked, somehow behaving as smooth as a snake charmer.

"Basically," I said.

"And which of Holt's annoying flaws brought this on?"

"Dude!" I said, momentarily forgetting the current problem.

Gabby rested her forehead against my shoulder, and if I had to guess, she was praying for strength.

"Gabby?" Darren asked.

She inhaled loudly before lifting her head. "Holt doesn't know anything."

"Oh," Darren sounded like he was holding back a laugh.

"Rick knows everything. He knows the rules and policies. Rick even knows people's names!" She took a shaky breath. "Like, real-world, life-or-death question: Holt, what's the name of the man who died?"

Oh, no.

Uhh...I should know that. I've heard his name a few times. Besides, in a way the man had saved my life.

"His name?" I asked, trying to buy time.

"Yes, Holt. His name."

Darren's eyes were wide. He knew I was in trouble, so he asked, "Why does *Geoff's* name matter?"

Gabby's throat made a displeased sound at Darren giving away the answer. "*Geoff's* name matters because Holt has one little idea, and suddenly my boss, Rick—my *real* boss—is terrified he'll be forced into early retirement because they want Holt to take over. Holt. A man who has to hear a name fifty times before he'll remember it."

"Wait, you wanted to make me look bad in front of the execs so they'd realize I wasn't management material?"

"That's right," Gabby said. "Rick was so worried about being fired, he barely ate and threw up any food he got down."

Really? Why hadn't I noticed?

The knife dug in again. One of these times she'd start drawing blood.

"You shouldn't have Rick's job."

Was Rick's job really what this was all about? "I don't want Rick's job."

"Really?" And Gabby almost imperceptibly relaxed.

"This was all about Rick's job?" I asked.

"Yes."

"That's a relief," I said—and strangely it was. "I thought you hated me."

"What? No, I don't *like* you, but I never *hated* you."

Darren's voice was slightly raised when he asked, "Then why did you plan to kill Holt during the speech Geoff gave?"

Huh? Oh, I guess Darren wasn't around when I figured it out.

"I didn't mean to." Gabby's voice went quiet.

"It was an accident," I added. "She just wanted to stop my speech, and Geoff was standing in the wrong spot when the light snapped."

"That's great," Darren said, and I think he was serious.

"It is?" I asked, as Gabby asked, "How?"

"Well, if you didn't mean to commit murder, his death wasn't premeditated. Manslaughter is way better than premeditated."

"That's true," I said. "People get accidentally killed all the time."

"Maybe not *all the time*," Darren said.

I rolled my eyes. With a knife digging into my back, Darren still felt the need to correct me. Gotta love lawyers.

The elevator dinged on the top floor.

For the first time the whole ride, Darren raised his hands. "What's the plan?"

"We'll all get out," Gabby said, but she didn't sound sure.

The door began to close, but Darren stopped it with his hand. "All you've done is pull a few little pranks. I'm sure everyone will understand."

My jaw twitched. That was a pretty big lie. Breaking into a restricted room to tamper with an elevator carrying people was a pretty big deal...not to mention the manslaughter.

"Don't confuse me," Gabby said. But she didn't move to leave.

"Darren would never confuse you," I said, then decided to roll the dice on sharing Darren's secret. "He loves you."

Darren's hand dropped from the door. It closed, and we began moving down to an unknown floor.

"You love me?" Gabby's voice was disbelieving yet held an undercurrent of hope.

Darren shoved his hands into his pockets, suddenly resembling a middle schooler. "I never said *love*."

"But..." I said, trying to get Darren to open up.

He swallowed, suddenly more freaked out than he'd been in the entire previous conversation. "But Holt's right. I was captivated by you from the moment I passed you in the hallway when you had your job interview."

"But that was nineteen months ago," Gabby said.

There was a softness I'd never seen on Darren's face as he said, "I know."

Hold on. Darren had been crushing on Gabby this whole time? Why hadn't I guessed it sooner?

"But you never said anything." The knife moved back so it was no longer pressed against my skin.

Darren shoved his hands deeper into the pockets of his Hawaiian shorts. "You were always so confident. I didn't want to slow you down." His eyes widened, and he swayed forward like he wanted to take the words back.

"And now?" Gabby's voice was so quiet, I wondered if Darren heard. "What do you think of me after seeing how I behaved in Phoenix?"

His jaw flexed. "Admittedly, committing manslaughter is a turnoff."

I raised my eyebrows.

Not helping.

"Come on, Gabby." Darren took a step forward. "Give me the knife. You don't want to hurt him."

The knife quivered as Gabby considered her options, and I flinched as the blade tore more of my dress shirt.

A ghost of Darren's million-dollar smile appeared, and for possibly the first time since meeting Gabby he let his feelings for her show. "Please, don't hurt my friend." He took another step forward. "I promise to get you the help you need."

One more step and Darren was right in front of us, holding out his hand for the knife.

Gabby's breath caught and I tensed, ready for anything. But slowly the knife left the spot under my blazer. "I'm sorry," she said as she handed it over to Darren.

I exhaled, and it felt like I'd been holding my breath since Gabby first got on the elevator. My vision grew grainy, and I gripped the railing. Had I been locking my knees?

"Don't pass out," Darren said.

I tried to glare at him. "I won't."

The elevator stopped, and an elderly couple got on and pressed the button for the ground floor. Darren held the knife discreetly by his thigh, and we all waited for the doors to open at the lobby.

CHAPTER 18

We called Detective Bunny.

Britt *didn't* slap Gabby.

The knife was handed over as evidence.

Gabby was arrested.

Darren and I gave our statements.

Then Darren attempted to thank Detective Bunny.

And after all that, my sister still expected us to go to an outdoor desert cowboy bar for dancing.

I'd handed over my button-up as evidence since Gabby had torn it with the knife. Plus a crime tech had taken photos of my back to record the scratches and red marks.

I just wanted to put on sweats and go up to my now safe hotel suite and watch TV until I fell asleep on the couch. But Juniper is a pest who never gives up, which is how I ended up sitting next to Darren on a bar stool while Britt and Juniper line danced on the outdoor dance floor.

As soon as we'd arrived, Juniper had ordered four tequila sunrises. My sister and my girlfriend quickly drank theirs before Juniper convinced Britt to join her on the dance floor.

Mine and Darren's tequila sunrises sat untouched. The drinks were too festive for our current moods. We sat brooding with glasses of whiskey. Chouzie's leash was tied to the bar, and he seemed affected by our glumness.

"Who was supposed to watch you?" Darren asked, his jaw tight with anger.

I raised an eyebrow, not sure what he was talking about.

"I told both of them you were never supposed to be alone, and you still managed to get cornered."

The darkness in Darren's eyes made me tread carefully. "Well, Juniper went outside, and Britt was in the lobby bathroom. I think the person who was supposed to watch me was...you."

Darren winced, but he didn't argue.

I took a gulp of my drink and let my eyes wander to the dance floor. My sister was in true form tonight. With her magnetic personality, there were now twice as many people dancing. But my eyes didn't linger on Juniper, instead focusing on Brittany. Her hair was loose around her shoulders, her cheeks were pink, and she was laughing.

I was glad she was having fun, but I couldn't bring myself to join in. I belonged next to Darren, who was arguably having a worse night than me.

"I've never seen her cut loose like that." Darren was also watching Brittany.

"Yeah, it's a side effect of spending so much time with Juniper. My sister"—I shook my head, remembering the time Juniper got me to dance on the dining room table—"wears everyone down eventually."

"Right." Darren picked up his whiskey and turned back to the bar.

I kept watching Britt dance, but I wasn't really paying attention. How could I have been so clueless to what was happening right under my nose? Darren was in love. Rick was sick over the possibility of losing his job. And Gabby was insanely loyal.

What about Brittany? Was she happy with me? Throughout the trip we seemed out of sync. Somehow I kept frustrating and disappointing her. What if the problem wasn't Phoenix, but went deeper? If I was messing us up, would I know before it was too late?

When the song ended, Britt ran up to me. Her eyes were shining as she came to stand right in front of me. Her hands went around my neck, and she was removing the lanyard with the conference badge, which out of habit I must've put back on when I'd changed into casual clothes. "If I put this on, will it make me official?" She slipped the lanyard over her neck and gave a pouty frown. "Now I'm serious."

I cracked a smile. "Very serious."

A new song started, and Britt began swaying to the music.

I hated to dampen her mood, but I had to know. "Britt"—I placed my hands on her shoulders and waited for her to stop moving—"are we good?"

"Uh..." Britt blinked. "Yeah. I think so." Her shoulders began moving as she resumed dancing, but I wasn't finished.

"Please." And my voice cracked.

Whatever was on my face caused Britt to transform into a serious paramedic. "What is it?" Her voice held none of the earlier teasing.

I shrugged. It was foolish to bring this up in a bar after a rough day.

"Holt?"

Brittany was tucking invisible strands of hair behind her ears. So far, all I'd succeeded in doing was making her nervous.

"I know I upset you this trip, but I don't know how much." I ran a quick hand through my hair. "I don't want to find out too late we have a major problem."

Britt nodded, her face analytical. "Okay. I understand." She stepped back, breaking our connection. I immediately missed her closeness. "This trip it became more apparent to me that you're not perfect."

She shrugged and gave a little smile. "But no one's perfect. I love you, and there's no one I'd rather be with."

"Hey, what do you mean *no one's perfect*?" I winked. "You're pretty perfect."

Britt laughed, and the brightness returned to her face. "Give it a few months."

"You'll still be perfect."

Before we could kiss, Juniper quite literally crashed into us. "You boys need to let your hair down." Juniper picked up my tequila sunrise, took a sip, then handed it over to me. "Here. Lighten up."

I frowned and set the drink back down. "Juniper, it's okay for us to be upset right now."

"Maybe. But"—Juniper tossed her hair—"I knew there was something off about Gabby and I warned you."

"No. You said she was in love with me."

"See!" Juniper pointed a finger in my face like I'd helped prove her point. "Loving you implies something off—no offense, Brittany."

"That's very offensive," Darren said from beside me. "There's nothing wrong with Holt. Well, there's plenty wrong with Holt, but nothing *wrong* wrong."

Wrong wrong? Darren was in worse shape than I'd realized.

"And Gabby..." Darren stared vacantly at the dance floor. "Gabby had a lot going for her."

Juniper snorted. "Sure. Aside from being a murderess stalker, she had plenty of good qualities."

"Be nice," I said.

"And you thought Gabby was hot," Juniper said, turning on me.

I shook my head. Even now my sister was trying to get me into trouble.

"Why don't I go back to the hotel," Darren said, finishing his whiskey. "I won't be much fun tonight."

"I'll go too," I said.

Brittany was starting to say, "Yeah, let's—"

When Juniper's "Nooo!" interrupted her. "Trust me. You can have a good time tonight. There'll be plenty of time to sulk tomorrow on the airplane."

"Juniper"—I leaned against the bar—"I'm really tired, and Darren had to arrest his long-term crush. Just let tonight be bad."

But Juniper shook her head. "No. I want Phoenix to be a good memory. Now drink your tequila sunrises and join Britt and me on the dance floor."

I sighed. Part of being tired was I didn't have the stamina to argue with my sister. So I asked, "Darren?"

He shrugged. "I'll dance if you dance."

Darren's eyes held a challenge. Juniper's were expectant. And Britt's—well, I could suddenly see she desperately wanted to dance with me. She wanted to share her joy of Arizona.

I shook my head, then picked up the tequila sunrise and waited until Darren had his. We clinked our glasses together.

"One song," I said.

"One song," Darren agreed.

Britt's lips trembled as she tried to hide her smile, but I knew this made her very happy.

A new tune was starting, and I grinned. "Britt"—my voice was low, just for her ears—"have you ever been swing dancing?"

Her eyes widened. "Have you?"

I nodded and held out my hand. "Are you ready?"

"For anything."

What's scarier? Skunks or Murderers? Read Holt's next mystery, _A Not So Happy Camper,_ to find out!

Ready for a Holt Jacobs snack-sized mystery? Sign up for my newsletter at _lilystirling.com_ and receive a copy of _Holt Jacobs & The Mystery Of The Missing Sunglasses,_ plus delightful every-other-week emails.

VICTORY!

Not only did Holt survive his work trip, but you also completed a book!

The years I spent working at a university sparked the idea for this story. While unconventional, I was sure Holt would thrive solving a mystery in a corporate setting.

I loved sprinkling in all the random team-building exercises that always happen during trainings—event organizers had to get us on our feet.

I love this book. So many parts of the book still make me laugh out loud. Did you love the story? It would really help me and potential readers if you rated and reviewed this book.

As you may have gathered from the breadcrumbs sprinkled in the story, Holt's next adventure takes place during a backpacking trip. *A Not So Happy Camper* follows Holt and Britt as they try to enjoy the great outdoors in the midst of solving a murder.

Want to hang out? Join my every other week newsletter at *lilystirling.com*.

You'll receive delightful updates and a copy of *Holt Jacobs & The Mystery of the Missing Sunglasses*—where he solves what happened to his sunglasses in a crowded airport.

Thanks for reading. It's been a pleasure!

Lily Stirling

ABOUT THE AUTHOR

Lily Stirling is the writer of the Holt Jacobs Mystery series.

She has spent a quarter of a century living in the Pacific Northwest. Lily was born in Idaho, but her family moved to Washington around the time she could read chapter books.

Mysteries have always delighted her, from listening to The Hardy Boys on car trips to watching episodes of Psych.

As for sarcastic families, when she's not writing about one, she's living in one.

Acknowledgements

I'm so grateful for everyone on my production team. Thanks for all you do!

Production Team:

Developmental Editor ~ Kristen Weber

Copyeditor ~ Penina Lopez

Cover Designer ~ Mariah Sinclair

—————◆◇◆—————

A huge thanks goes to my family for all your love and support. You're wonderful listeners, readers…and occasional conspiracy theorists—always ready to make suggestions on future stories.

To my author friends Bellamina Court and Jess Corbeau, I'm so happy to be a *Moonshine Girl* with the two of you. I can't imagine lovelier people to write a book series with. I'm looking forward to when the rest of the world can read *Murder & Moonshine*.

Thanks to Alessandra, Terezia, Eva, and my author friends at Inkers Mastermind. It's been incredible to have such a supportive writing community.

Finally, thank *you* for reading my book and all the back matter. I hope you love *A Not So Simple Seminar* as much as I do!

Until next time!
Lily Stirling

HOLT JACOBS MYSTERY SERIES

A Not So Shocking Murder

A Not So Rustic Retreat

A Not So Rosy Vintage

A Not So Cozy Christmas

A Not So Simple Seminar

A Not So Happy Camper

———◄O►———

Holt Jacobs isn't for everyone. He's a sarcastic introvert who can never get quite enough coffee. Becoming a sarcastic sleuth was unexpected, but as an engineer, Holt is used to solving puzzles.

MOONSHINE GIRLS MYSTERY SERIES

Murder & Moonshine

————————⬤O⬤————————

Moonshine Girls Davie Carter, Fenn Everhart, and Daisy Mae Harper met over moonshine and have been friends ever since. They'd planned on distilling, transporting, and selling illegal hooch but keep stumbling over crimes and solving mysteries.

————————⬤O⬤————————

The Moonshine Girls Mystery Series are intertwined anthologies written by Lily Stirling, Bellamina Court, and Jess Corbeau.